TRIAD

TRIAD

THE TRIAD SERIES, BOOK 6

KATE PEARCE

Copyright © 2017 by Kate Pearce

All rights reserved. Without limiting the rights under copyright reserved above, no part of this publication may be reproduced, stored in or introduced into a retrieval system, or transmitted, in any form, or by any means (electronic, mechanical, photocopying, recording, or otherwise) without the prior written permission of both the copyright owner and the above publisher of this book.

This book is a work of fiction. Names, characters, places, brands, media, and incidents are either the product of the author's imagination or are used fictitiously. The author acknowledges the trademarked status and trademark owners of various products referenced in this work of fiction, which have been used without permission. The publication/use of these trademarks is not authorized, associated with, or sponsored by the trademark owners.

1

<hr>

QUOXOR PROVINCE, PAVLOVAN

RAIN DATTA EASED HER HEAVY KIT BAG OVER HER SHOULDER AND approached the ticket booth, sliding her I.D. card across the counter.

"Good morning." Rain said politely.

The male leaned as far away as possible as he swiped her card.

"I need a ticket to the Neveks region in Quoxor Province," Rain continued. "I should have credits in place from the military. My number is—"

He pushed the card back using one fingertip. "I can't help you."

Rain frowned. "You do operate a service out there?"

"Yes." He glanced briefly at his screen. "Once a month. You just missed it."

"It was supposed to run today." Used to the vagaries of transportation outside the major cities, she tried again. "If I've missed the direct bus, there must be a way to get to Neveks using other routes, right?"

"Nothing that I can offer the likes of *you.*"

His sneer this time was loud and obvious.

"Hang on a minute," Rain said, holding on to her temper by a thread. She'd already had a long day and was in no mood to make it worse. "Are you discriminating against me because I'm from Neveks? What *century* are we in?" She jabbed at her uniform. "I've served in the Pavlovan military!"

He still wouldn't look directly at her. "There's no point getting annoyed with me, female. I don't make the rules. Due to new regulations regarding native tribes in this region, I'm not allowed to sell you a ticket without prior authorization from my manager, your current employer, and the Neveks authorities. According to my systems your name isn't on *any* of those lists."

Rain let out a long slow breath. "This is *ridiculous*. What am I supposed to do now?"

The clerk shrugged.

"I'll buy her ticket."

The voice came from behind her, and she swung around to stare up at the unknown male. He was tall and had striking pale blue eyes and a hard face.

He nodded at her briefly, and then returned his cold gaze to the ticket seller. "No member of the Pavlovan military should be denied a seat on a public bus. I'll buy two tickets."

"You can't—"

"Get down!"

In a blur of motion, Rain was swept off her feet and rolled to the ground. From within the cradle of the man's arms, she watched as a large vehicle careered off the side of the road and came spinning down the bank toward the bus station, brakes squealing, horn blaring. It swung around in a slow, perfect arc, almost as if it was a vidmovie, and took out half the building as well as the two empty buses waiting for passengers to board.

"Wow." Rain breathed through a mouthful of dust.

There was a horrendous crashing and tearing of metal, and then everything shuddered to a stop. Rain pushed herself free and stood up, coughing in the smoke, and tried to assess the damage. It was early in the morning so there weren't many people around, and she could see no obvious casualties who needed help. She cautiously lowered her telepathic shields. No one appeared to be hurt.

The clerk leapt to his feet and pointed straight at Rain.

"You did this! You caused this, Thought Stealer, Mind Thief!"

Rain didn't bother to answer, but grabbed her pack, turned away, and headed out. It looked like she'd be walking, so she might as well get started before it got really ugly around there. Gradually the smoke and the dust settled behind her, and she breathed clean air. She could hear sirens and emergency vehicles and wondered whether the clerk would be dumb enough to send the authorities after her.

It wouldn't be the first time someone from Neveks was arrested for simply being in the wrong place at the wrong time.

"Hey."

She'd known someone was following her, so she wasn't surprised at the shout. It was a shame the military hadn't allowed her to bring her favorite weapon home, but she was trained in hand-to-hand combat so she could still hold her own. She didn't stop walking, but slowed enough to let the tall male come alongside her. It was the guy who'd offered to buy her a ticket and thrown her to the ground like a real hero.

"You still planning on going to Neveks?"

During her military service she'd met people from all over the planet, but his accent was unfamiliar and his mind…was like nothing she'd ever encountered before. She slowed down and faced him.

"Of course."

He studied her carefully. "How are you planning on getting there?"

"I've got these things." She pointed at her feet. "I'll walk."

"You don't want to share the cost of a rental?"

"A what?"

"A hired vehicle."

"No one in this town would rent me anything."

He raised an eyebrow. "Why's that?"

This time she stared at him for quite a while, but he didn't appear to be joking. "Because I'm from Neveks."

"The ticket guy called you a mind stealer. Does that have something to do with it?"

"Are you super slow or what?" She jabbed herself in the chest. "I'm from *Neveks*! We can read people's darkest thoughts and sub thoughts and bonded-Triad thoughts. Nothing is safe from our horrible, devious minds."

He regarded her impassively. "So what am I thinking right now?"

"You…are just weird." She started walking again.

"How?"

She spoke over her shoulder. "I don't have time to play games."

"I can't sense you in my head, so you're obviously not that powerful."

"You *can't*?"

He shrugged. "Nope. I have excellent shields."

"That usually doesn't matter." She stopped again. She couldn't sense him, which was remarkably soothing. "You're not from around here, are you?"

"I'm from planet Earth."

She gave him her best don't-fuck-with-me look. "They don't have telepaths there, Earth man."

"It's hu-man, and let's just say it's an emerging talent." He hefted his backpack higher on his shoulder, his expression calm. "Are we walking or not?"

SHE SHRUGGED, which Jay took for assent, and he fell in beside her. He could sense her in his head just fine, but as long as she wasn't aware of it, he was good.

"How long do you reckon it will take us to get to the Neveks region on foot?"

"A week if the weather stays fine and you don't hold me up." She didn't bother to look at him. "I know a few shortcuts off the main route."

"You've done this before?"

"You heard the man at the bus station. We're not popular, so most Neveks learn to have a backup plan."

"That sucks. I don't think I've met anyone from your region before."

That was the truth. The fact that he'd spent a month studying up on her culture, and all data available on her personally, was another matter entirely.

"That's because most of my people stay home." She sighed. "Which kind of makes anyone who *does* venture out into the world even more conspicuous and even less welcome. Why are you going to Neveks?"

"I'm actually heading for the Temple of Quoxor. I've got a big decision to make about my future, and that seemed like a good place to think it through." That was another truth. "I'm not particularly religious or anything, but your Oracle does seem to have some extraordinary powers. I've heard it's a great place to meditate, and I know one of the palace security team out there."

"She's not my Oracle. Neveks worship their own Queen Goddess who rules over our tribes."

"You don't go to the temple to find your Triad members?"

He knew most of this already, but he was trying to get her to trust him, and acting like the stranger in town was the best option available.

"No."

Damn. She sure wasn't chatty.

For a while she said nothing as they moved off the main highway and crossed into a wooded area. It was cooler under the trees and much quieter. He studied the unfamiliar trees and birds, his keen eye cataloguing each new sight and storing it in the A.I. database that masqueraded as his brain. Information came back to him, detailing which creatures were dangerous, which could be eaten, and which were poisonous.

He paused as a big blue bird laboriously flapped its way from one branch to another. His companion stopped as well, her face turned up to the filtered sunlight, her gaze everywhere. Her hair was black and tied at the nape of her neck, her eyes were as green as the foliage, and her skin…it was like watching a kaleidoscope in motion. Whatever she came near was reflected back in the changing shades of her melatonin.

"You're staring at me again," Rain said.

"I've never met someone from Neveks before." He shrugged. "You're like a chameleon."

"A what?"

"It's a creature we have on Earth that can change the color of its skin to avoid predators. I bet they loved having you in the military."

"They tolerated me." She smoothed a hand over her throat. "I had my uses. Are you military?"

It was only the second direct question she'd asked him. He wondered how much she could pick up despite his enhanced shields. It was one of the uncertainties about the Neveks telepathic reach he'd been directed to investigate.

"I was in the army on Earth. I was sent here with the Oracle's heir." He resumed walking and risked a question of his own. "Why are you going to Neveks?"

"My mother is ill. I've been given permission to visit her."

Jay pretended to consider her answer, even though he knew exactly where the permission had come from. "Why do you need an invitation? Aren't you going home?"

"I was kicked out when I was eighteen." This time her impatience showed on her face. "Can we keep walking? I'd like to be out of this wood before it gets dark."

"Sure, sorry. It's just nice to have someone to talk to, you know?" He glanced down at her unresponsive expression. "I've been traveling by myself for four weeks already."

She didn't ask him anything about his journey or himself, which was fine by him. He didn't like lying, and if she was prepared to tolerate him tagging along while he attempted to gain her trust and entry into Neveks? That was good enough for now.

"My name's Jay. What's yours?"

"Rain."

"Like the weather or like a queen?"

"The weather I suppose." She shrugged. "I didn't pick it."

"It's nice."

She gave him an eye-roll for that bit of pandering, and he stopped talking.

The scene at the transit center had been carefully staged to make her notice him being heroic. When the bus careered toward them, he'd relied on his enhanced hearing and speed to get her out of harm's way. Not that she'd acknowledged his derring-do. She'd simply stood up, brushed herself down, and disappeared in the crowd. He'd already guessed from the speed with which she'd vanished that she was pretty good at taking care of herself, but at least he'd managed some kind of an introduction.

He dug in his backpack for his water bottle and held it out. "You want some?"

"I've got my own, thanks."

He'd told her that he couldn't sense her thoughts, but that wasn't true. Like all telepaths on Pavlovan, she gave off a subtle signal that resonated with his enhanced senses. When he and the other guys had first arrived from Earth, the sound of that collective psychic energy had been a balm to their much-abused systems. It was only the second time in his life when he'd actually felt like he belonged somewhere.

"Do people from Neveks form Triads like the rest of Pavlovan?"

"Yeah."

"But without the help of the Oracle?"

She shifted the strap of her backpack onto her other shoulder. "The Queen Goddess makes the decisions."

"All of them?"

"Pretty much." She glanced up at the angle of the sun. "We should keep walking for another hour or so, and then stop to eat. It gets steeper from here in as we follow the path through the mountains."

"Which is your polite way of telling me to shut up and keep moving." He surprised a quick smile out of her, which she quickly covered with a frown. "Lead on. I'll try and keep up."

She increased her pace, and so did he. He could walk for days without stopping, but she didn't know that, and he didn't want to make her suspicious. He'd monitor her body for signs of fatigue and match whatever she did. It was possible that she might try and evade him for reasons of her own. No matter what happened, he was sticking to her like glue. She didn't know it yet, but the very future of planet Pavlovan might depend on it.

"ARE WE GOING TO STOP SOON? I'M GETTING TIRED," JAY CALLED out from behind her.

Rain waited for him to catch up. They'd been climbing steadily upward through the foothills of the Quoxor Mountains. The path was narrow, and the incline made her calves burn. To be honest, she was exhausted herself, but she'd gotten into the rhythm of walking and completely forgotten about the time and place. She turned a slow circle, her senses on high alert.

"There's a river bank down to our right. Let's set up camp there."

True to his promise not to bother her, Jay had walked behind and kept the pleasantries to a minimum. It was weird being so close to someone and not being bombarded by thoughts and sub thoughts all the time. She'd even relaxed her formidable shields a little, which was unheard of.

He groaned. "No fancy hotel?"

The warmth of his teasing reached her telepathic senses, and she immediately shut him out again. "They probably wouldn't rent me a room. Not that I have the credits for it, either. Something's up with my financial information."

"If we get desperate, I'll rent a room, and you can pay me back your share later, okay?"

"Sure, but I don't think we'll be stopping off in many towns along the way. Neveks are not encouraged to mix with the general population."

"I'd heard that it was the other way around. That your people don't want anything to do with the rest of Pavlovan."

She set her pack down on the riverbank and rolled her aching shoulders. "There are some elements of the community who feel like that, but not everyone. "

"Why wouldn't anyone want to move with the times and get out more?"

"Because when my grandparents were children, their parents were forced to hand over their offspring to be educated by the Pavlovan State in special 'integrated facilities' hundreds of miles away from here. You can imagine how well that went down."

"That's terrible." Jay grimaced as he wiped the sweat from his forehead. "They tried some stupid shit like that on Earth a few centuries ago. It was a disaster." He sat down beside her and stretched out his legs. "Gods, I'm tired."

She couldn't help but notice how fit he was. His damp T-shirt stuck to his flat stomach, and his muscled thigh was way too close to hers. He wasn't an obviously bulked-up guy, but he was super fit. She moved slightly away, and he made no move to follow her.

"At least we don't need a fire. I think I'd melt." He groaned and stood up again. "I need water. I have purification tablets in my kit."

"The water is drinkable here."

"Not if you're from Earth." He winced. "Trust me, I found out the hard way. I'm told I'll get used to it eventually."

He ambled down to the river while she sorted out her sleeping roll and pillow. She had enough food to last her seven days. After that, she'd either need to find a store that would serve her or start hunting. She eyed her companion. He was crouching down beside the water, filling up a container. He might be able to buy food for them. She would pay him back.

A yawn shook through her. She'd barely slept since she'd signed out of the military camp two days ago. Could she trust this 'human' enough to sleep beside him? If she wanted to be one hundred percent safe, she'd have to drop her shields a little so that she'd be alert, and that might cause a whole other set of problems. Pavlovans tended to react in two ways to a Nevek mind probe—either they loved the sensation or hated it. Neither reaction was comfortable to the average citizen, so the Nevek people had learned to turn inward, to build their shields, and to keep everyone out.

A whoop made her turn back to the river. The human had stripped off his clothes and jumped in. She couldn't help but smile at his exuberance and the faint hint of telepathic joy emanating from him. He wasn't from Pavlovan. Was it possible that his apparent indifference to her abilities meant he wouldn't notice if she kept a telepathic watch over him all night?

"You coming in?" He yelled at her. "It's great in here."

She shook her head and sorted out her rations. She hoped he had his own food. He looked like he'd eat a lot.

She finished setting up camp and sat down to watch one of the two suns setting behind the Quoxor Mountains. Her companion emerged from the water and walked toward her with the easy gait of a predator. He was completely naked and she couldn't help noticing he was lean, muscled, and extremely well-hung.

She quickly averted her gaze and fiddled with her water heater. She was actually blushing, but with her skin color it was hard to notice. He slicked a hand through his short hair and shook himself like a *canis*.

"That was really refreshing." He turned his back on her to

rummage in his pack, giving her a nice view of his world-class ass. Normally she didn't allow herself to check out males because a hint of interest from someone from Neveks usually sent most Pavlovans into a hysterical frenzy. Maybe because Jay was human, he wouldn't respond that way or even notice she was looking.

He climbed back into his pants and T-shirt and sat opposite her, using his towel to finish drying off his hair. His pale blue eyes were an unusual color and unheard of for someone from her tribe. She'd watched a vidmovie at the base once about shapeshifters on Earth who transformed into wolves, and his eyes reminded her of that animal—highly intelligent and a true predator. She was right to be wary of him.

He grinned at her. "Do you want something to eat?"

She indicated her rations. "I'm good, thanks." Good manners made her ask, "Do you have food?"

"Yeah. All I need is some water to heat up this crap." He poked the bag and pulled a face. "It's not great, but at least it has the required nutritional elements."

"I have a heater."

"Awesome." He checked his water bottle. "This looks good now. You heat yours up first. I can get more water if we need it."

They ate together in companionable silence, rinsed off their utensils, and settled in for the night. Rain's thoughts flew to what she would find when she was finally home. When the request from her mother had come through, and permission had been granted for her visit, she hadn't believed it was true. No one was allowed back into Neveks after being banished. The explanation that somehow her outstanding military service had made the application successful didn't sound right to her. The Queen Goddess must have approved her return.

That alone gave her pause, because the Queen had more reason to keep her away than anyone. Maybe the visit might be allowed, and her death would be the price paid for it. Rain let out her breath and squeezed her eyes tightly shut. Maybe death would be worth it just to see her mother again.

She would not think about that. She would enjoy the journey with her strange offworld companion and worry about things beyond her control when she finally got there.

13

3

"There's a town up ahead." Jay pointed it out to his companion.

They'd been walking alongside the banks of the river for three days, following it upward until it became a stream and then disappeared altogether. Now they stood at the top of a rocky outcrop, looking down into the valley below where the lights of a small town twinkled and glittered in the dusk light.

"Yeah. So what?"

Jay had become used to Rain's laconic answers. She kept everything to the minimum, barely bothering to check he was still following along. But he'd noticed a slight lessening in her shields and the guards she'd set against him, which suited him fine. She had no idea that his brand of telepathy had been designed to infiltrate the toughest of defenses.

He deliberately slept close to her at night, letting her see he wasn't a threat, hoping that she'd ease her shields back just a fraction more because they were straining even his powers of concentration. What he hadn't anticipated was the physical effect the rest of her would have on him...the sound of her breathing, the warmth of her body stretched out beside his.

He'd forgotten there was an intimacy in sleeping next to someone.

She smelled good, like the frosted chocolate cake his mother used to bake for his birthdays. He didn't remember the actual date of his birth anymore.

It didn't bother him. His mother had ended up hating him, and he wasn't the same person. He'd been reborn, reforged, whatever you wanted to call it. He shouldn't be reacting to Rain because he had a job to do, but it was vital he kept her happy. He was known as a cold-blooded operative and needed to get a grip fast. He studied her. Would she be happy if he tried to seduce her?

He suspected she might shoot him with his own weapon. He would normally be the first to admire her self-sufficiency, but not right now when he needed some leverage over her.

"We could get a room." With a grimace he shifted his backpack from one shoulder to the other. "I sure would like to sleep in a real bed for a change."

"I'm not stopping you." She started down the trail, her ponytail bobbing as she walked.

"If I can get us in, will you share it with me?"

"They won't give me a room. We're too close to Neveks. They all hate us around here."

"Why? I don't get it."

She turned back to face him, her green eyes full of shadows. "Because some of my ancestors didn't behave themselves too well and raided this area, subjugating people's telepathic abilities and turning them into mindless slaves who could never escape Neveks."

"Wow, what a sucky thing to do."

"It all sucks, but that's how it is. You learn to live with it, or you die." She almost stumbled on the uneven, rocky surface, and Jay grabbed her arm. She raised her gaze from his fingers to his face.

"Careful."

She scowled at him. "Let go of me. You move too damn fast sometimes."

"I can't help that." He stayed close. "Look, let me at least try, okay? We're both worn out after that rain and could do with a cleanup."

He'd deliberately pushed her over the past two days, knowing she wouldn't admit to fatigue, and feeling none himself.

She pushed her hair away from her face. "*Okay.* Just do what you want! I'll hide outside, and you can let me know where I'm supposed to go."

RAIN LEANED back against the wall and fought the temptation to fall asleep. She was used to hard physical work, but the pace Jay had set over the past couple of days had been blistering. She pictured his austere features and the powerful energy that emanated from his hard, muscular body. There was something wrong with him... He moved too fast, his mind was just strange, and he was being way too nice to her. Gods, she was so tired...

She contemplated the leaden skies and the steep rise out of the valley she'd have to get over to reach the Nevek territories beyond. She could just forget about her strange companion and move on.

Would he come after her? She suspected he might. He'd probably run her down with that relentless stride of his, toss her over his shoulder, and...

What would he do then? Tie her up?

She thought about him looming over her, his taut body and those strange hypnotic blue eyes focused solely on her...

Rain shivered. She was too damned tired to do much more than breathe. And in a weird way, being around someone whose thoughts she couldn't access at will was remarkably soothing. His lack of contempt for her was also a balm after her years in the military.

"I'm getting soft," Rain muttered to herself. "He's definitely after something."

But what if this was the last journey she ever took? The chance that the Queen of Neveks would have her killed was fairly high. Couldn't she just enjoy sleeping in a bed occasionally? Not being hated? Being warm and safe?

What if he wanted to sleep with *her*?

She blinked hard at the unexpected thought. He'd never given any indication that he was attracted to her, but there was something going on between them. Some weird telepathic vibe that she didn't know how to deal with because every relationship she'd ever had with a male had ended badly.

The door to the motel office opened, and Jay came out. He spotted her immediately and made a strange gesture with his thumb, which she took for a positive sign. Making sure that there was no one watching, she followed him around to the back of the building to a single block of rooms. He paused and then headed for the last one in the row.

By the time she reached him, he'd put the lights on and closed all the blinds. As she closed and locked the door behind her, the warmth engulfed her, making her shiver. Jay glanced over and raised his eyebrows.

"Why don't you take the first shower?"

"Thanks, I will."

Rain took her time, luxuriating in the plentiful hot water before wrapping herself in a towel and doing a bit of hand washing of essentials in the sink. It was so nice to be clean again. Putting on the fan, she went out into the main room, closing the door behind her.

"It's all yours."

He was standing by the desk, using some kind of tablet. His

cold blue gaze swept over her, lingering on her body. She raised her chin and let him look, but it didn't seem to faze him either way.

"I've ordered dinner."

"Real food?"

His sudden smile surprised her, making her rethink his attractiveness, and then wonder why it mattered to her.

"Yes. If I'm still in the shower when it turns up, knock on the door and let me know, okay?"

"So you think it's best if I stay hidden?"

"Not for my benefit, I assure you."

He strolled toward her, and she tensed, suddenly aware that she was in the presence of a healthy male who was causing an intense physical reaction from her, which was unheard-of from a person from Neveks. By shedding her clothes had she revealed too much of herself? Was he telepathically projecting his interest or was she noticing it for the first time while they were shut up together in a small space?

Rain clutched at her towel, making sure it was still in place as he paused in front of her, his breath fanning her throat. Her stomach knotted, and she shivered.

"Here." She blinked as he reached past her into the bathroom, grabbed a robe from the back of the door, and gave it to her. "Stay warm."

She managed to nod as he shut the door behind him. She found her way to a chair. What the *frek* was going on? Sure, she'd become steadily more aware of him as a male as they'd traveled together, but she wasn't supposed to be sexually aware of anyone except a fellow Nevek.

But Jay was different. He wasn't even from her planet, so maybe the normal rules didn't apply. She couldn't even say whether she liked him or not, seeing as she'd made no effort to actually get to know him beyond the basics. He was calming to be with. He seemed to like her without being afraid, and that was so…refreshing.

She rubbed a hand across her eyes. She was so tired maybe she was imagining things. After all, what had he actually done? Looked her up and down like any male and been helpful by handing her a bathrobe. But that wasn't all, was it?

He was dangerous. He wasn't *right*. She would do well to remember that.

She padded over to the side of the bed farthest away from the door and sat on the edge, moaning with sheer pleasure at the softness of the mattress beneath her. Memories of her mother's house and the scent of her baking made her close her eyes…

"Room Service!"

Rain jerked awake and ran over to the bathroom to knock on the door.

"He's here."

There was no answer, so she opened the door to a cloud of steam and waved a hand through it before stepping inside.

"Dinner's here." Rain went still as she registered that Jay was naked and still in the shower. Soapsuds ran down over his perfect abs as he washed his hair.

She swallowed hard as he suddenly looked right at her.

"Got it."

Without even bothering to grab a towel, he sauntered past her, reversing their positions and gently closing the bathroom door in her face, which at least gave her time to breathe. *What was going on with her?* She would have to ditch him somehow and go on alone. This indecision—this craving to get up close and personal with a male she didn't completely understand or trust—was *insane.*

Decision made, she leaned against the door and contemplated when to disappear. The lure of hot food and a bed for the night were hard to resist. Maybe she could leave early in the morning when both of them should be sleeping off their fatigue.

"You can come out now," Jay called from the bedroom.

She made sure the bathrobe was secure and went into the other room. In her absence, Jay had pulled on a pair of boxers and a T-shirt, which made looking at him a lot easier.

He gestured at the table, which was covered in trays. "I got a selection of stuff. I didn't know what you liked, but I noticed you don't eat much meat."

Rain sat down, her stomach rumbling as she tried to take in all the amazing aromas at once.

"Neveks don't eat meat, and I never got to like the taste of it even after I left." She reached for a napkin and spread it over her lap. "Do you like the food here? Is it different from where you come from?"

He was looking at her funny, probably not used to her actually asking him something. She was suddenly a bit ashamed of her attitude toward him. It wasn't his fault that she was somehow attracted to him.

"It took some getting used to," he acknowledged as he reached to uncover some of the dishes. "But I'm military. We ate a lot of prepackaged unidentifiable shit anyway. Probably blew out my taste buds years ago."

She sighed as he handed her a plate filled with food. "That looks so good."

"Here you go. Eat up."

She didn't need a second invitation and dug into the pile of fragrant *lacheck* and assorted steamed vegetables. They both ate quickly for a while, and then Jay slowed down, his attention fixed on her face.

"What's up?" She paused to stare at him.

"You're making this humming noise through your nose."

"It means I'm happy, and the food is good."

"Yeah?" He raised his eyebrows. "It sounds like you're having sex."

"Oh, I'm much louder when I'm having sex."

He reached for more food. "I'd like to hear that."

Rain went still. "Are you coming on to me?"

His smile was strained. "If you have to ask, I'm obviously out of practice. I haven't had sex since we landed on this planet."

"And how long ago was that?"

"Over a year ago."

She gazed at him until he leaned over and used the tip of his finger to close her mouth. "It's okay. There's no need for you to say anything. From your stunned expression, I guess I've got my answer. I haven't exactly been the best companion have I?"

Rain swallowed hard. "I thought that was my fault."

He shrugged. "You have every right to protect yourself from a stranger—especially me. I'm not easy for you to read, and that must make you suspicious. And you know what? Having sex with you is a bad idea. I'm not sure why I even said that when we've got nothing in common, and we're going our separate ways in a few days." He wiped his mouth with his napkin. "How about you forget I mentioned it and enjoy your meal?"

"Are you trying to confuse me now?"

"No, I'm trying to stop acting like a colossal dick who allowed the sight of you moaning over a plate of food to override a decade-long instinct to keep out of trouble." He shoved a hand through his hair. "I'm the ice man. I'm the closed-off guy, and you…just make me want things I don't deserve."

He rose to his feet. "I'm going to walk over to the office and check the local weather."

"You can do that right here," Rain pointed out.

"I know." He gave her a brief smile as he stood up. "Keep eating. I'll be back soon."

JAY LET himself out of the room and walked around to the side of the motel complex. What the fuck was wrong with him? He had a mission. The last thing he needed to do was get *involved* with that mission and risk her turning him in when she realized what he'd done—if he managed to do it. There was only one thing to do—check in with the boss.

"I'm in trouble."

The voice of his commanding officer came back to him. *"What's up?"*

"I want to have sexual relations with the female you asked me to follow into Neveks."

"What the fuck?" Kaiden didn't sound pleased. *"There's a reason I sent you and not one of the others. You've got the best shields and defenses, so how the hell is she getting to you? Is it deliberate? Is she onto you?"*

"I don't think she wants to be attracted to me either, but there it is." Jay hesitated. *"I'm trying to be honest here, Commander."*

"Then tie a knot in it until we're sure she's not involved, okay? Fuck her brains out after the mission is completed."

"But what if our intelligence is correct, and she's got no more idea than we do how she's going to be received in Neveks? She's the first person in years who's been allowed back in there."

"Captain Roberts, this is a life-or-death, save-the-whole-fucking-planet kind of gig we've got going here. There is too much to risk just for you to get laid."

"I get that, sir." Jay took a deep breath. *"In that case I think you'd better send someone else. I'll just say goodbye to her tomorrow, pretend I'm taking another route, and you can take it from there."*

"There isn't anyone else!" Kaiden snapped. *"You know that. I need you to focus and get this done, okay?"*

"I'll do my best. Over and out."

Jay glared down at his hard cock. It would be better if he got a separate room, but then the motel guy would wonder why one person needed so much space and would probably come and investigate. He squared his shoulders. Kaiden was right. The fate of Pavlovan might rest on what he discovered in Neveks. He couldn't afford to mess up.

With that resolve firmly in his head, he turned back to the motel and decided to take a long, slow, wet walk around the perimeter.

There was no sign of Rain when he finally reentered the room. The dishes had been left outside the door, and all the leftover food was piled neatly onto two plates set on the table. She emerged from the bathroom, stopping when she saw him.

"Are you all right?"

He blinked at her. "I'm fine."

The swirling colors of her skin intensified, which he had begun to realize meant she was embarrassed. She shoved her wet hair behind her ear. He hadn't realized it was so long until she'd washed it.

"I didn't mean to run you out of the room you paid for. If anyone should leave, it should be me."

He leaned back against the door, fighting the stupid impulse to bridge the gap between them, take her in his arms and fuck her brains out. "It's raining out there. We have two beds. Let's just go to sleep, shall we? I promise you I'm too tired to try anything."

"So am I." Her smile was hesitant. "Okay. Let's do that."

RAIN WOKE up to darkness and blinked hard. Her skin was on fire, and she was sweating like she was trekking through the heat of the jungle. She pushed her covers down to the end of the bed, sat up, and drank an entire glass of water. She never got sick, so what was happening?

"You okay?"

Jay's voice reached her through the blackness.

"I'm just hot."

"Do you want me to turn the air-conditioning on?"

"No, I'm sure I'll be fine in a minute."

She closed her eyes and concentrated hard, seeking out the problem within herself, but couldn't identify the cause. It felt like she was burning up, and she couldn't lie still. Had she caught some Earth virus from the human?

"I don't get sick," Jay said quietly.

She grimaced. If he could access her thoughts, she was really in a bad way with no energy to maintain her shields.

"Why don't you get sick?" Rain tried to distract herself. "You're just a mass of contradictions, aren't you?"

"Yeah. I suppose I am." He hesitated. "I'm a product of an experiment—a super-soldier project that ended up creating a breed of telepathic killers that scared the crap out of their creators."

"Is that why you had to leave your planet?"

"If we hadn't had left with your Goddess in Waiting, we would have been executed."

"That's terrible," Rain said.

"We thought so, but we could also see the problems we had created."

Rain breathed out slowly as her temperature lowered. "Because you were too dangerous to exist? That sounds like how most Pavlovans view the Neveks."

"You were born like that. It's hardly your fault, is it?" His voice hardened. "I volunteered because I was a cocky, overconfident idiot who wanted to be a hero."

"But you didn't know what you would become, what they would turn you into, did you?"

"They never tried to hide the fact that it was a risky experiment. I wanted to be superhuman. I *wanted* those enhanced abilities and telepathic powers." He sighed. "But there is a price to pay for everything, right?"

"And what price was that?" Rain asked softly.

"Losing my family and my sense of self. Beginning to see myself as some kind of Godlike killing machine."

Rain considered his harsh words. "I don't get that from you at all."

"Because you're blocking me out. Trust me, if you let your shields down, you'd run away screaming."

"I doubt it." Rain shivered as a wave of sweat cooled on her skin, and drew the covers up again. "I've been in the military for years. I've experienced way too many of my fellow soldiers' thoughts in combat to balk at anything."

"I'm barely human anymore. I kill, and I move on." His voice was implacable.

"So why are you visiting the Oracle? I got the impression you want to change something in your life?" Rain asked.

He was quiet for so long that she thought he'd drifted back to sleep.

"I want to know if there's any hope for me."

"Hope for what?"

"That I can somehow find a balance between what I've become and what I once was—a purpose that maybe doesn't involve indiscriminate killing and no remorse."

"Find the male within the warrior," Rain mused. "That is a worthy quest." She turned toward him in the darkness, her own problems temporarily forgotten. "I wish you well with your journey and your quest for balance, human."

"Thank you. I wish you well with your journey, too."

"Mine is slightly different." For the first time ever Rain allowed herself to reveal the purpose of her journey. "I have been allowed back into Neveks to say goodbye to my mother who is dying."

"Forgive my ignorance," Jay said slowly. "But I thought you said that once you were expelled from Neveks, you could never go back."

She didn't remember telling him that, but she answered anyway. "You can't. I was granted a special dispensation by the Queen Goddess."

"Is she a connection of yours?"

Rain shivered. "No, I think she hates me. I suspect my life will end shortly after my mother's."

"Then why risk going back?"

"Because I haven't seen my mother for ten years, and I want to say goodbye."

"Would *she* want that?" Jay persisted. "Would she want your life to be forfeit for hers?"

"Because I returned to see her on her deathbed?" Rain smiled into the darkness. "She would consider it my fate and would accept it as she accepted my banishment. The Queen's word is not only the law, but a spiritual edict that cannot be denied."

"Fuck that."

Rain blinked and sat up. "What did you say?"

"I said fuck her. Why should your life be subject to the whims of a Queen who prides herself on isolating her tribe from the rest of the planet?"

"It is to keep the bloodlines pure. Hers especially." Rain was fairly certain that was why she'd been banished in the first place, but had no proof of the matter. No one had dared to contradict the Queen; even the one person she had assumed would speak up for her. "I was eighteen. I was hardly in a position to argue with the whole tribe."

"And now?"

"What do you mean?"

"If the Queen orders your execution, will you go willingly or will you fight?"

Rain sank back onto her pillow and contemplated the ceiling. Thank the Goddess the horrible overheated sensation had receded, leaving her feeling wide-awake and hyperaware.

"It depends."

"On what exactly?" Jay demanded.

"On what I find when I get there."

Goodness, he sounded extremely angry on her behalf, which was something that had never happened to her before. Speaking to him in the darkness was proving remarkably easy. She'd never revealed so much about herself to any male before.

"If you're convinced you're going to die anyway, then why not take a few of them down with you?" Jay persisted.

He was all warrior now, his voice cold, emotion repressed.

"Because some of them are...my family." She sighed. "You must think me weak."

"Not at all. I am amazed that you can be so compassionate about a society that threw you out to fend for yourself at such a young age."

"I hated what the Queen did for years." Rain curled her fist into the blanket. "It *ate* at me, fueled my anger, and made me the soldier I am today. The suspicion and dislike of my fellow Pavlovan warriors was nothing compared to what I'd lost and endured from my own people. Eventually, most of them came to accept me as one of them, and that meant more to me than anything."

"So you gave up your anger and now are going meekly home to be slaughtered."

"Possibly," she admitted it at last.

He snorted but didn't say anything as it occurred to her that in less than a week she might no longer exist.

"I could come with you," Jay suddenly said. "Guard your back. Get you out of there safely."

Unexpected tears filled her eyes. Dammit, she never cried, and here she was about to lose it because a self-confessed callous killing machine was offering her his protection and help.

"I'm fast, and I'm impervious to Neveks mind tricks. We

could be out of there the moment things got complicated." Jay said.

"Thank you." Rain just about managed to reply. "I cannot accept your kind offer, but I appreciate it more than you could ever know." For the first time in her life she let down her telepathic shields with someone who wasn't from Neveks.

Thank you.

After a tense moment, his guards relaxed, and their minds flowed together in harmony, soothing and completing each other in the most unexpected ways. She closed her eyes and just enjoyed the moment. The last time she'd had such an experience had been just before she left Neveks.

"I want you." Her thought crystallized and poured into his receptive mind, gathered his immediate response, and came back to her.

"Yes."

"I cannot promise more than this one night, but I would like to share it with you."

His response was to leave his bed and come to hers, the mattress sinking as he settled beside her.

"Is this because you think you are going to die?"

"Yes."

He leaned in and kissed her mouth, his touch so gentle it almost brought back her tears.

"I haven't had sex since I arrived on Pavlovan."

She smiled against his lips. *"Then you probably are in need."*

He groaned and kissed her again, the tip of his tongue traveling the seam of her lips, seeking admittance, which she willingly gave to him. His kiss was a revelation—it was as if he already knew her, as if they were meant to fit together for all eternity.

"I don't want to hurt you," Jay murmured.

"You won't."

He framed her face with his callused hands, his fingers threaded through her hair, his pale blue eyes intent.

"I lied."

"About what?" Rain went still.

His smile was crooked. *"I actually stopped having sex back on Earth. I was afraid I might...damage someone—that because of my enhanced physical strength that in the blindness of climax I'd inadvertently hurt them."*

"Did you ever actually do that?"

"No." He slowly exhaled. *"But I came damn close."*

She reached up to cup his chin. *"I trust you."*

"Then I will try to be worthy of you." His mouth descended again, and this time he didn't hold back; his kiss claimed her and ignited the long suppressed fires within her skin. While they kissed, his hands roamed over her body, learning her curves and secrets, making her strain against him in a wordless plea for more.

Grabbing his hand, she placed it between her legs, moaning as his fingers skimmed over her swollen, wet welcome and slid deep. She came almost immediately, and he groaned her name, doubling his presence within her, pushing her even higher.

He shoved his knee between hers, spreading her thighs wide so that he could settle between them, the hard ridge of his wet cock already pushing against her stomach.

"Please..." She dug her nails into his shoulders, urging him closer, bucking her hips to help him angle his cock right where she wanted it.

"Too...fast." Jay groaned.

"No, just right." She eased her heel up the side of his flank and planted it on the muscled cheek of his ass. *"Now. Do it now."*

He reared back and then drove forward, filling her in one juddering, slick motion, her body clinging to his, giving way and welcoming him into her hot, wet core.

She started to come, and he went rigid, his teeth clenched,

his jaw set as he fought his own climax until she stopped thinking, and he stopped fighting, and they came together in a scalding meld of mind and body that Rain had never imagined existed.

He collapsed over her, breathing hard, which amused her immensely. Wasn't he supposed to be the superior physical being? With a soft sound, he rolled them both over onto their sides.

Rain lay beside Jay and breathed him in, enjoying their mingled sweat, the telepathic high they were currently sharing. She was reluctant to break such perfect harmony. She wasn't supposed to feel like this about anyone who wasn't from Neveks. Maybe the Queen had been right all along, and she wasn't purebred.

"She cast you out because you weren't pure enough?"

Jay's question cut through her happy buzz.

"That's what she said. I went for my confirmation ceremony at eighteen. She proclaimed the Goddess had spoken to her, and I was not worthy to have a Neveks mate or a life with those who were chosen."

He kissed the top of her head and wrapped her in his arms. *"That must have been devastating."*

"Yeah."

"And yet you're still intending to go back."

"I have to see my mother."

"Then I'm coming with you."

She opened her eyes, stared right into his, and spoke out loud. "No. They'll kill you."

He shrugged. "They are going to kill you anyway, so we might as well go down together."

"Jay…" She squeezed his shoulder. "Just because we've done this, doesn't mean you have to sacrifice yourself for me."

His mouth set in a hard line. "I have no intention of sacrificing either of us."

She blew out an exasperated breath. "It's easy to be terribly overconfident when you have no idea what facing the Queen Goddess is like."

He bent his head and kissed her again. "How about we stop worrying about the future and focus on where we are now?"

"But—"

Her protest turned to a gasp as he licked his way down to her breasts and set his teeth on her nipple. His cock swelled inside her, and she allowed herself to get lost in the pleasure of his mind and his touch once again.

4

RAIN WOKE UP AGAIN AS HEAT ENGULFED HER. SHE EXTRICATED herself from Jay's arms and padded over to the bathroom. The light came on as she entered, bathing her in a cold, white glow. Something was very wrong. Her skin was itching as if she'd walked through a poisoned forest. Was it possible for her to be allergic to a human's semen?

She took the quickest, coldest shower of her life, and stood shivering on the mat while she carefully dried herself off. She hissed as her fingernail caught her skin and studied her hand. Her nails were literally growing as she watched them, curling into dangerous claws.

"This can't be right," she said slowly.

She rushed to the mirror just as her jawline stretched, and her eyes widened and turned black. Her only thought was that she had to get out of there. Had to find somewhere to hide until whatever was happening to her—the thing that should *never* have happened to her—went away.

Jay thumped on the door. "Rain? What's going on?"

She opened her mouth to order him to stay away, but actual

speech had deserted her. She spun around, looking for an escape. If she saw him, if he saw *her*...

"Rain!"

Jay disabled the lock and ran into the bathroom, coming to an abrupt stop as he saw the figure crouched in the corner. *What the hell?* The defensive mechanisms that masqueraded as part of his brain booted up, sending him directly into fight-or-fight mode.

"*Get out!*" Rain growled.

Jay literally pinched himself to make sure he wasn't still in the middle of some ghastly nightmare. Rain's face was turned away from him, but the whole shape and color of her body looked different. There were small ridges growing up her spine, and he caught the flash of fangs as she tried to avoid the light.

His A.I. flashed a warning through his brain. "IMMINENT DANGER. RETREAT."

Even as he choked back his disbelief, the analytical part of his intelligence kept working, cataloguing the changes in her, sensing her body temperature, the scent she was now giving off, and gauging the level of danger. His A.I. might be telling him to run or kill, but all that was human in him was screaming to just focus on her smell and the siren-pull of her mind.

One piece of information lodged in his head and kept repeating itself like a Greek chorus. No one had ever witnessed a Neveks triad couple mating. It was a rite shrouded in secrecy. *No one* had seen this, but the probabilities calculated in his brain that she was in some kind of mating state were inescapable.

"*Get out, or I will hurt you.*" Rain's guttural warning echoed through his skull and the tiled bathroom.

The thing was, he couldn't look away, couldn't escape the

bond they'd already forged. Inside her, she was still Rain, and his stupid fucking body and mind couldn't ignore that.

"No," Jay said.

She hissed at him, drawing herself up to her full height. Her skin now resembled ancient armor or an exoskeleton, her eyes were wide and black. God, she did have fangs. His cock kicked up. Typical daft bastard. He sent up a quick prayer to all the deities known and unknown in the universe and took a wary step closer.

With a roar, she leapt for him, and he caught her around the waist, avoiding the snap of her fangs with a deft flick of his head. Even in this new form she was still Rain; he could sense her telepathically.

She let him roll her onto her front and kicked him so hard in the shins that he almost came down on top of her. Even as he attempted to avoid crushing her with his weight, she flung herself to one side, making him crash to the floor, and made for the outer door. He couldn't let her go outside. She'd create a massive incident, and all his cover for the ongoing investigation would be blown apart.

Struggling to his feet, he launched himself at her retreating figure and brought her down again, centimeters from the exterior door. Her claws scratched down the paintwork with an excoriating sound, leaving gouges in the wood. Reaching over her head, he fused the lock system, so the only way out would be through the barred window or busting through the door itself. And neither of those things was going to happen on his watch.

God, she smelled delicious, like anger and a shot of pure adrenaline combined with the mind-blowing aroma of raw sex. For a vital second he wrestled with her, needing all his superior speed and strength to even contain her. He wished there was some kind of manual for how to have sex with someone from

Neveks. He was damned if he knew how to get past those fangs and body armor.

He set his A.I. diagnostics to work on a battle plan, even as he wrapped his fist in her hair and flipped her over onto her back.

"You're not going anywhere, Rain."

"Frightened. This isn't supposed to happen to me."

"I get that, but I'll do anything you need, so use me, take me."

"I might KILL YOU."

"No, remember?" Jay braced himself to stare at her face. *"I'm a super soldier. You can't kill me."*

For a long moment she stared at him out of her elongated, alien eyes. Then she snarled and flipped him over like a pancake to straddle his lap.

"Wait—" Jay croaked, but it was too late.

She lowered herself over his cock, and he forgot how to breathe as her clawed hands kneaded and stroked over his body, sending all his nerves into a sexual frenzy. He lifted his hips, offering her more, and she took it, bending down to him, her fangs grazing his throat, her tongue emerging to play with his.

So this was how you had sex with an armored Neveks female.

She was still Rain. They still had the same telepathic connection that made him want to fuck her brains out—if she didn't eat his first. He wrapped one arm around her hips, eased back until he was leaning against the wall, and planted his feet on the floor.

"Go for it."

With a hiss she rocked her hips, arching and writhing above him like a beautiful golden dragon. He watched, entranced, and then had to concentrate on not coming as her internal muscles gripped and milked his cock with every sinuous undulation. He set his jaw as she rode him hard, pushing back after every downward thrust, giving her what she needed.

And her need was...*spectacular*. Rain mixed with something

so alien and yet so elemental—it was like fucking the source of the universe. She tightened around him and climaxed with a roar that wasn't human at all. He could do nothing but come with her, setting his jaw, and fighting back his own primeval howl in case the neighbors complained.

She fell against him, her breathing harsh and distorted by the overlap of her fangs over her lips. He tentatively ran his hands over the ridges on her back, wincing at the sharpness of the fish-like scales, but enjoying the texture and difference. She should have wings. She could fuck him in midair, and then let him fall to the ground, his cock torn off when she was sated like a queen bee.

"Fucking beautiful," he whispered.

She growled in his ear, reminding him of a pack of wolves he'd once seen in the northernmost section of Earth.

She'd been thrown out of Neveks for not being pure. Had the Queen decided Rain was not able to transform to mate? Was this ability central to the Neveks race? Rain seemed horrified that she had it. Jay sensed his questions would have to wait until Rain returned from her more primal state. *If* she returned... All he was getting from her at the moment was the need to fuck, and he was more than happy to oblige. For the first time since his strength had been enhanced, he knew that whatever he did wouldn't be too much for a Neveks female in heat. He wouldn't be surprised if she needed two males to satisfy her. All he could hope for was to survive the experience.

She climbed off him, grabbed him around the throat, and, with one easy motion, threw him across the room and onto the bed. He righted himself almost immediately. She followed him down in a tangle of arms and legs as they fought for dominance. She went down on her knees, and he crowded her against the headboard, one hand wrapped in her long hair, the other at her waist, and thrust into her from behind. Her ridged scales jabbed into his chest and belly like a thousand spikes. She hissed and fought him, but he kept her pinned and hammered into her, forgetting caution and restraint—all the things that had made him give up sex before. She could take him. She *wanted* this. She needed this.

As he filled her, he slid one hand around to play with her clit. She bucked even more, arching her ridged back to let him slide deeper. He set his teeth at her throat and increased his pace beyond human speed and endurance. He forgot everything but the connection with Rain's incredible alien mind.

For the first time in his life, he wondered if he was going to run out of come. Before he could test the theory, Rain shoved him off her, and he fell onto the mattress, bouncing from the strength of her maneuver.

She crawled toward him, snarling something unintelligible, and bent her head over his cock. He groaned as her long hair caressed his spread thighs, and then caught his breath as her fangs grazed the length of his dick in a pain-pleasure that made him moan her name.

She nipped his hipbone and then settled over him again, swallowing his throbbing length inside her before going still. Jay gazed up at her, seeking the spark of her humanity, and saw nothing but "other." She still looked magnificent, but there was no sympathy or compassion left in her eyes.

Maybe she really was going to eat him alive…

"Oh crap," he muttered as she swooped down on him, setting her fangs in his throat and piercing his skin. He climaxed in a shuddering, hot wave, and then everything went black.

<hr>

RAIN WOKE up tangled in damp sheets with every part of her body—even her jaws—hurting. Had she come down with some kind of virus? She cautiously opened one eye and inhaled the overwhelming scent of sex and sweat and….

Mate...

With a whimper, she forced herself to sit up and stumble over to the other bed. Jay lay naked and flat on his back. His whole body was marked and bruised, and his throat was bloody. His eyes were closed, and he didn't react when she touched his face.

She found his pulse and tried to count it even as she shivered and shook like a frightened child.

"Dear Goddess..." she whispered. "What have I done?"

5

She'd fucking run away from him...

Jay dragged himself out of the shower and got dressed. Every part of him felt like he'd gone ten rounds with a snarling leopard and lost. A wave of dizziness came over him, and he forced a couple of protein-pack meals down his throat. He could track her through their telepathic link. He also knew where she was going, and his strength would soon return.

He refused to think about what he'd do when he caught up with her—either fuck her brains out, or murder her. Maybe both. She'd probably like that. He also tried not to think about what Kaiden was going to say when he heard what had happened. If he reconnected with Rain and completed his mission, maybe he'd be forgiven.

Jay grabbed his backpack, laced up his boots, and moved out. God knew what the staff would make of the ripped, blood-stained sheets and damaged furniture, but maybe they were used to that kind of shit, being near Neveks. She'd joined with him. They'd shared an unforgettable experience, and, whatever happened, they needed to talk about it. He'd keep his shields high and hope she didn't detect his presence, but he'd find her.

He had no choice.

As Rain headed into the forests surrounding the walls of Neveks, it began to pour, making the terrain even more difficult to traverse and her temper more uncertain. She'd morphed. There was no getting away from it. She'd been told she couldn't morph because she was impure and that she couldn't mate in the traditional way with a Nevek male because her blood was tainted. Yet she'd gone into the deep mating state, albeit with a male from another planet.

The Neveks Queen had some explaining to do, that was certain—if Rain got a chance to see the Goddess on earth. She might settle for just killing the woman rather than bothering to get an answer. At eighteen her world had ended, and she'd been cut off from everything and everyone she knew and loved. Ten years had passed, and it still cut like a knife.

A bird called somewhere deep in the steamy forest, and Rain raised her head. She was getting close to the outer defenses and had probably been picked up on the sensors. Not that she cared if they knew she was coming. She'd been invited.

Even as the thought entered her head, another bird sounded off, this time right above her head. She barely had time to look up before a net dropped, and she fell to the ground, enmeshed in its coils. A man knelt over her and grinned.

"Welcome home, Princess."

It was the last thing she saw before he knocked her out cold.

Breathing hard, Jay entered the clearing to see a group of hunters gathered around a net. He considered his options. He was fairly certain they had Rain, which meant he could simply follow them and work out how to get into Neveks. Or he could unleash the unexpected torrent of rage he was currently experiencing because they had *dared* to touch his female. He wanted to kill every single one of them—

"Don't move or I'll gut you."

Jay briefly closed his eyes as a knife pricked his throat. The mating thing was messing with his internal sensors. He had to calm down. One of the males tossed Rain over his shoulder and jogged off into the forest toward the walls.

"I don't want to hurt you," Jay said evenly.

Even as the man laughed, Jay was in motion, his hand coming up to break his captor's wrist and force him to the ground.

A sudden shout had him whirling around to see the rest of the hunting party advancing on him. He hesitated, unwilling to kill, but ready to do whatever it took to get to Rain.

"Foreigner," one of the men spat at him, his golden eyes narrowed. "What do you want here? Go home."

"You took my woman." The words tore from his throat. Hell, he had nothing to lose, they could kill him right now, or he could massacre all six of them before they even knew what was happening.

The tallest man jerked a thumb toward where Rain had been carried off. "*That* woman? She's Neveks."

"She's mine."

A blitz of telepathic activity battered against Jay's shields, and the man bowed. "Then, you will accompany us."

Jay nodded as the male behind him grabbed his arm and shoved him forward. He had a sense that he was in for a rough journey. If it got him inside Neveks, and he was still alive, he'd accept any punishment they meted out to him.

RAIN REGAINED CONSCIOUSNESS, slowly opening her eyes. She was in the women's quarters of the temple. Her clothes, weapons, and backpack had disappeared. Her head hurt, and she wanted to throw up. Rolling onto her side, she leaned over the edge of the bed to find a bucket ready and waiting for her use.

Exhausted, she lay back, and someone placed a cold cloth over her brow. After another long moment, she pushed the cloth away and forced herself to sit up.

"I want to see my mother."

"Of course." The female who wore the yellow silk of a junior priestess and healer bowed her head. "As soon as you are recovered, I will take you to her."

"Thank you." Rain looked around the lavishly furnished room. She'd once lived on the temple grounds with her mother and was familiar with its layout. If she was correct, she was currently lodged within the Royal House itself.

"Is the Queen Goddess here?"

"I am not at liberty to share that information with you," the priestess said. "I will fetch you some sustenance and then take you to your mother." She hesitated. "She does not have long to live."

"So I understand."

At this point, Rain was just glad that her mother was still alive to see her. When her mother died, she was the last of Rain's kin. No consequences would befall her family if she decided to put an end to the Queen Goddess.

She dutifully ate the food put in front of her and enjoyed the juice of the local *quor* fruit she'd helped her mother pick when she was a child.

After washing her hands and face in the bowl of scented water the priestess offered her, Rain smiled at the woman. There was no harm in trying to disarm the opposition and make them think she was harmless.

"May I see my mother now?"

"I will call the guard." The priestess nodded. "Remember that you are a guest in our temple, and thus will behave accordingly."

"Trust me, I have no desire to stay here at all," Rain said sweetly.

Before the guard entered, Rain was offered her choice of silks to wrap herself in. She chose blue, the color of the warrior guild. It felt weird not to have on underwear. Her skin was marked from her mating with Jay, but she was neither ashamed of that, nor worried that anyone would notice. She'd been banished at eighteen for being impure. No one would suspect she had morphed and mated or even care if she had. She was a nothing, her name erased from the records, her image deleted…

The guard came in, and she recognized him as one of the hunting party from the forest. He bowed to the priestess, and then nodded to Rain.

"Please come with me."

He took hold of her elbow and marched her between the all-too-familiar honey-colored pillars of the temple. The smell of incense and the murmur of prayer floated around Rain, calming her raging thoughts.

Where was Jay? Had he recovered from their mating? She suspected he'd be mad as hell about her leaving him again. But maybe not—maybe he'd run screaming in the other direction because she'd morphed into a monster.

The guard took her through to the healing wing, where the soft incense was replaced by the harsher smells of medicines, cleanliness, and the sharp metallic taste of death. She steadied herself at the entrance, deliberately shutting down all her emotions, and consolidated all her power into her shields. If the Queen Goddess did turn up, she would get nothing from Rain except death.

She only faltered when she reached her mother Alaya's room, fighting feelings she could not afford to show.

"Mother."

The guard positioned himself at the door and let her go forward alone. She knelt by the side of the low pallet and stared down at her mother. Even at rest, Alaya's skin was tight, flat, and yellow, not reacting at all to her environment. Pain radiated from her emaciated frame and her lank, dark hair was streaked with silver

"She has the wasting sickness. She will soon pass over to a better world."

Rain looked up to see a nurse sitting quietly in the corner of the room, her face sympathetic and her tone firm, as if daring Rain to argue with her. She didn't need to protest. Her mother's condition was obvious. Even her telepathic shields were gone, which for a person from Neveks was the ultimate humiliation.

"Rain?"

A whisper drew her attention back to her mother.

"Mother."

"You came back."

She found a smile from somewhere. "Yes. The Queen Goddess gave me permission to visit you."

Alaya grabbed her wrist and whispered, "She is not to be trusted."

She kissed her mother's fingers. "I will do my best not to enrage her."

"She will kill you this time."

"I'm a trained soldier and much harder to frighten than my eighteen-year-old self." Rain tried to sound more confident than she felt.

"I begged her not to banish you."

Rain swallowed hard. "That is in the past. I survived my banishment, and I'm here with you now."

"To watch me die."

There was no point in offering false hope, but it was hard for

Rain not to try. It was not the Neveks way. Her mother had her faith and would not regret passing to a better world.

"You will perform my funeral rites, Daughter?"

"Of course." Rain gathered her courage. "I will be with you right up until the moment the Supreme Being takes your hand and walks with you into paradise."

"Thank you. That is all I ask." Alaya closed her eyes. "Will you stay with me now?"

Rain glanced up at the nurse, who nodded.

"Yes. I will be here until the end."

Her mother gave a relieved sigh. "Now tell me everything you have been doing since I saw you last."

BY THE TIME they threw him into the cell, Jay was bloody and bruised but not quite broken. It had been hard not to fight back to his full capacity, but he didn't want them to know they'd captured an enhanced soldier quite yet. They were already suspicious of him. He set his back against the wall opposite the door and settled in to wait. At some point he'd either be fed or interrogated, and his gut wasn't expecting a meal any time soon.

He wasn't sure if it was something in the walls that surrounded him, but he could hardly sense Rain. Her shields were at one hundred percent and nothing he had tried so far had penetrated them. He knew she was somewhere within the complex, but that was about it.

"YOU SHOULD NOT HAVE ENGAGED IN COMBAT IN YOUR CURRENT WEAKENED STATE."

Hell, even his A.I. was nagging him now.

Had Rain's mother died yet? He leaned back and closed his eyes, needing to regain his strength, but wary of letting his guard down. Inside him was a conflicting mess of raging emotions fighting against his installed A.I. It was crucifying him. Was Rain okay? Surely he'd know if she was dead. He'd feel it in his soul…

He must have dozed off because the crash of the door being unlocked and opened woke him. He peered through the gloom as the guard came in with a lantern.

"Visitor for you, foreigner."

Jay stayed where he was and looked up at the huge male who'd entered behind the guard. He was a head taller than Jay and possibly twice as wide, with rippling muscles that flexed and flowed beneath the reddish brown of his kaleidoscope skin. He wore some kind of checked garment that bared one shoulder —it reminded Jay of a Scottish plaid—and carried a dagger at his side.

Jay braced himself as the male attempted to breach his shields and then abruptly stopped.

"You are something of an anomaly, aren't you?" Despite his warrior-like appearance, his voice was surprisingly melodious and calm. "I cannot read your mind at all." The huge man crouched in front of Jay, his head tipped to one side. "Why is that?"

Jay shrugged and then gasped as the male's hand shot out and wrapped around his throat.

"My name is Asar. I am in charge here. You *will* answer me."

As his vision blurred, Jay's A.I. calculated his odds of survival. He decided to cooperate.

"I'm from Earth," he wheezed.

Asar's grip eased a fraction. "Earth? Where is that?"

"It's another planet in a different galaxy."

"With telepaths?"

Jay nodded as best he could.

"Yet you laid claim to a woman of Neveks."

"One cannot lay claim to another person," Jay objected.

The male released his grip on Jay's throat. "One can, if one is part of a bonded Triad, yes?"

"We don't have those on Earth."

"Then what is your interest in this female?"

"We traveled together. I was worried when your thugs in the wood captured her. I thought if I said she was with me then I'd be able to find out why she'd been taken."

"Worried…" Asar regarded him with an unconvinced smile. "You injured one of my men and demanded we release your woman. Surely that implies ownership?"

"Not in my world. I said what I needed to get in here, and it worked, didn't it?"

"You wanted to come into Neveks?"

"No, I *wanted* to make sure Rain got here safely before I continued my journey to the Temple at Quoxor, where I am *expected* by Captain O'Neill, the First Mate of the Oracle's heir."

"You have friends in high places."

"Who will come looking for me if I don't turn up soon." Jay met the male's piercing amber gaze. "Once I've made sure Rain is safe, and determined whether she wishes to continue on to the temple or remain here, I promise I will leave quietly."

"That decision is not up to you." Asar rose from his crouch and loomed over Jay again. "It is in the hands of the Queen Goddess, as is the fate of Rain."

"Rain's fate is her own."

Asar's mouth quirked up at the corner. "She is certainly an outlier."

"You know her?" Jay risked the question, but the male's face closed up. "Just let me see her and then I'll leave or do whatever is necessary to get out of your way."

Asar was almost by the door and looked back over his shoulder. "I will consult with the Queen Goddess."

"Great."

"When she returns."

"And when will that be?"

Asar shrugged. "Who knows the plans of the sacred ones?"

Jay frowned. "Then let me see Rain. I'll leave before the Queen Goddess needs to even be bothered by my petty presence."

"No one leaves or enters without the Queen's permission," Asar said flatly.

Jay tried another tack. "Will you just confirm that Rain is here?"

"If you're a telepath of some kind, you must know if she is."

"And is she still in good health?"

Asar raised an eyebrow. "You fear she will be harmed by her own people while she prepares her mother for death?"

Jay didn't answer but continued to stare right into Asar's eyes. He was beginning to get a sense of the immense telepathic power behind the male's sturdy defenses.

"Be very careful, foreigner. We respect the rituals of death in Neveks," Asar murmured. "And remember the Queen Goddess can kill you with a thought."

With a final nod, he exited the cell, and the door was locked behind him. Jay let out his breath.

Whoever the man was, he emanated power and, in his weakened state, Jay had struggled to keep him out of his head. He wanted to find Rain now and get out. After the ferocious mating and the recent beating, his body refused to comply. His A.I. calculated his odds of survival were low if he attempted a breakout. Everything was off, and he had no energy.

He'd sleep, regenerate, and be ready to fight the next day.

6

Leaving her mother to sleep, Rain stepped out of the bedchamber and walked straight into the guard posted outside the door.

"I wish to pray." She looked up at him. "You cannot deny me that comfort."

"As you wish." He took a step back and waved for her to precede him. "Remember, I will be at your side the entire time."

"I expected nothing less," Rain said.

It was strange walking along the familiar hallways, with the soft silk of her robe catching the slight breeze. Would Jay even recognize her out of her military fatigues? Even as she thought about him, a stab of concern lodged itself in her chest. He wasn't dead. She was somehow certain she would know that, so where was he? Instinct told her that he would have followed her to Neveks and that he was somewhere close.

She paused at the entrance to the women's side of the temple and removed her sandals. The familiar ritual was soothing, and the prayers came back easily to her mind. She lit a candle and walked into the center of the large space where there were cushions and benches to kneel on that faced the high altar. The walls were a soft rose-pink and hundreds of candles covered every available surface.

The snarling Goddess who guarded the altar was so ancient that no one knew exactly when she had been carved from the local stone. Her original color was lost now, buried beneath layers of what had once been blood sacrifices, now abandoned. In the old days, anyone from Neveks who had failed the Queen Goddess's test at eighteen had been sacrificed on the altar. Maybe Rain's banishment had been a blessing in disguise.

Keeping her gaze lowered, Rain approached the altar and carefully placed her candle among the others before backing away. She knelt down at one of the benches and closed her eyes, allowing the peace and tranquility of the sacred place to wash over her. She'd gotten here in time to see her mother. That was the most important thing. Now all she had to worry about was her own death and what would happen to Jay.

Clearing her mind, she proceeded to pray for her mother, asking the spirits to be kind and to give Alaya a good death with little pain and suffering. She wasn't sure she believed in the Supreme Being right now, but she was willing to try anything to help her mother.

A vivid picture flashed in her mind of Jay slumped asleep in a cell, and she opened her eyes. Was he here? She gently dropped her shields as far as she dared and caught the jumble of his thoughts. He was in pain. He was worried about her…

A graphic flashed across the void and embedded itself in her head. It showed Jay's damage report and rejuvenation estimates, presumably calculated by the A.I. in his brain. Had she gained access to his innermost thoughts because they had mated? Could she communicate with it?

"AFFIRMATIVE."

Rain blinked at the answer and tried to form a response. *"Tell him I'm all right. Tell him to leave if he can."*

"DAMAGED."

"But you can help him rejuvenate, right? Then tell him to leave peacefully."

"MESSAGE RECEIVED."

Rain winced and hastily raised her shields. She checked to see if anyone was coming, but she was still alone. It was possible that the temple had been cleared so that her contaminated presence wouldn't affect the true worshippers.

She hoped Jay would leave… If she saw him again she had no idea what she might do. Leap into his arms or run in the opposite direction? She felt more connected to him than ever, and, seeing as she could access his A.I., she had to suspect that the unusual bond went both ways.

There was the sound of voices beyond the doorway. Rain stiffened and then rose to her feet. If trouble were approaching, she would rather face it head on. She went to the door and washed her hands before walking out into the connecting corridor.

Her guard had gone, but there was another large, all-too-familiar male awaiting her.

"Greetings, Rain."

She briefly closed her eyes before pasting on a smile. It was inevitable that she'd be forced to meet the one man she had hoped never to see again in her lifetime.

"Asar. I was hoping you'd died."

The flash of surprise on his face at her unconventional greeting made her want to cheer. She was no longer a gently born eighteen-year-old who thought herself in love. She had nothing to lose and a whole lot of things to get off her chest before someone killed her.

He bowed. "Unfortunately not, although, in truth, it is *your* survival which is the bigger surprise." He straightened up and looked her over. His eyes were light brown—almost yellow—and they were full of appreciation.

Rain refused to be the first to look away. "Fortunately for

me, the Queen Goddess only banished me rather than sacrificing me on that altar in there. That's the only reason I survived and was able to become a soldier."

A flash of distaste crossed his face. "You joined the Pavlovan *military*?"

She raised her chin. "An honorable occupation by most people's standards. Not everyone chooses to hide within their own walls on this planet, Asar."

"But—"

"I had *nothing*. No money, no family, and nowhere to live. The military were the only people who would take me in. Would you have preferred it if I'd died on the streets?"

He frowned. "I hate to doubt your words, but *no one* from Neveks is banished like that."

"How the hell would you know?" she said sweetly. "I was the first person banished in a generation. As I recall, *you* had a convenient hunting trip that week so you didn't have to see me leave. Now, will you excuse me? I have to get back to my mother."

When she tried to edge past him, he grabbed hold of her elbow. "Your mother is in excellent hands. Let's finish this conversation, shall we?"

She pulled out of his hold. "This conversation was finished the day I left, and you did nothing to stop it."

"Exactly. You *left*."

He looked as furious now as she felt, which was a small victory. If she was going to die anyway, she might as well go down having settled all her old scores.

"What's the difference, Asar? I was *gone*, wasn't I?"

"A banishment is a sacred act that no one can interfere with." He folded his arms over his massive chest. "*Choosing* to leave because you defied the Queen Goddess is another matter completely."

"Wow. You sanctimonious *pig*." Rain shoved him in the chest.

"*What* did you just call me?" Asar asked. "*You* attempted to overthrow the *Queen*."

"Is that what she told you?" Rain regarded him for a long moment and laughed. "Great, whatever. Believe her, because the fact that you *chose* to says everything about you and what a sham our relationship was."

He drew himself up to his full, impressive height. "She is the Queen Goddess."

"And your *mother*. The Gods help you."

This time she managed to get past him and strode furiously along the corridor to where her guard awaited her.

"Take me back to my mother's room, please."

The male looked over her head to where Asar was standing and obviously received the nod to proceed, which infuriated her even more.

"This way, Princess."

"And stop calling me that!" she snapped. "I am no longer a citizen of Neveks. I have no rank here, and I don't want one."

***

ASAR WATCHED as Rain strode away from him, her head high and her shoulders rigid. She was as beautiful as she had always been, but now her face had more character, and her eyes…

She had seen more of the world than he had done and somehow survived it.

What had she meant about his mother deceiving him? He couldn't believe she had the nerve to criticize the Queen Goddess. Rain had left because *she'd* fallen out with the Queen and tried to kill her. The shock of returning from his hunting trip and discovering that the female he was certain he was bonded to had abandoned him had broken his heart.

But Rain had just laughed in his face, her expression a challenge, her whole body taut with dislike and mistrust when he'd suggested she'd lied. When his mother had agreed to his plea to allow Rain to visit her dying mother, he'd imagined *her* finally apologizing for abandoning *him*.

Despite his mother's urgings, he had never ventured into the sacred temple again to ask about his destined mates. If the Gods had lied to him about Rain, then why should he believe they would offer him another mate without the promise of a completed Triad?

Rain was *his*.

Just seeing her again, inhaling her scent, feeling the familiar tug of her telepathic signal, had set all his buried senses alive.

Asar considered what his mind and body were telling him. If Rain *was* his mate, then had he been at fault by not challenging the Queen Goddess's decision to banish her? Was it possible that his mother had been *wrong*? But, like her sister Oracle at Quoxor, the sacred vessel was n*ever* wrong.

If Rain was not of pure blood as his mother had insisted, then even if she'd stayed he could not have bonded with her. As the Queen's only son, it was his duty to procreate to produce more female heirs. But why had he been attracted to Rain if a bond was impossible? The more he thought about it, the more confused he became.

And what claim did the male currently locked in the dungeons below have on Rain? Despite his desire to get rid of the stranger in the quickest and most expedient way possible, he couldn't simply kill him. The male claimed to be friends with the Oracle's heir at the Quoxor Temple and had this strange connection with Rain.

Asar slammed his palm against the door. Nothing made sense anymore.

He could only hope his mother returned soon and helped him understand the complex mess. It was unlike her to be away for so long. He'd wondered whether she had chosen to avoid seeing Rain again, but couldn't imagine why. She was a

Goddess. If she couldn't explain what was going on, then there was no hope for anyone.

———

"Take me to see the male in the cells." Rain demanded imperiously. After a restless night's sleep, she'd had breakfast with her mother and left her resting quietly while she attempted to get around the guard.

"What prisoner would that be?" The guard looked at her warily.

"The one you brought in just after I arrived. He is my traveling companion and should not be held like a prisoner."

"If you are so concerned for his welfare, why didn't you mention him sooner?" the guard retaliated.

"Because I didn't realize you'd been stupid enough to catch him until after I regained consciousness!" Rain met his gaze. "Let me see him."

"I cannot do that, Princess. I don't have the authority."

"Then take me to someone who does."

He sighed and turned on his heel. "As you wish."

She wasn't surprised when the guard took her to Asar's set of rooms. In his mother's absence, and with no female heir, he was the highest authority in the land. When she'd fallen in love with him at sixteen she couldn't believe her good fortune—that the Queen's son wanted her—that they had a telepathic bond...

Had he seriously believed she'd left him in a fit of pique, or tried to overthrow the Queen?

What a loser.

"Rain." He rose from his chair with a fluid grace unusual in such a large man and bowed to her. He wore a simple tunic of green silk and his long hair was tied back from his face at the nape of his neck. "What a pleasure. May I offer you some refreshment?"

"No, thanks."

"How is your mother this morning?"

"The same." Rain shrugged. "She is unlikely to recover, but I think she appreciates my company."

"As do we all." Asar inclined his head to her.

Rain allowed her skepticism to show on her face. "I'd like to see your prisoner, please."

Asar waved at her guard to withdraw and returned to his seat. "Why?"

"Because we were traveling together. I feel responsible for his wellbeing."

"Is that all?"

She smiled. "It's all that has to do with you."

"You have changed greatly in the last ten years." He sighed. "You are much…harder."

"Yes, being banished and serving in the military will do that to a person. May I see Jay please?"

He stayed seated, his head angled to one side. "My mother said you tried to assassinate her in the Temple."

Rain fought back several replies and finally settled on something that wouldn't get her immediately thrown into the cell *next* to Jay's. "And you *believed* her?"

"At the time, her reasoning seemed adequate." Asar watched her carefully, his mind reaching for hers until she telepathically slapped him down.

"You don't get to pretend to bond with me anymore," Rain said. "So keep your thoughts in your own head where they belong."

Asar stood and towered over her. "I never *pretended*."

"Right." Rain looked back at the door. "Now can I see Jay?"

He took hold of her elbow. "I did not *pretend*."

She tried to shake off his grip. "And I'm not here to talk about the past, but to see my mother and help my friend. Got it?"

Asar held on, his amber eyes staring into hers, his *touch*…

"Let me go," Rain said softly.

His smile held a hint of victory. "You still feel me and know me. You cannot deny it."

"Take me to Jay," Rain repeated her demand, unwilling to admit that touching him had shaken her to her core. She still responded to him, which wasn't helpful, and, worst of all, Asar was completely aware of it.

"As you wish."

ASAR WALKED in front of Rain as they descended into the almost empty palace dungeons. He'd motioned the guard to fall in behind her. Not that he thought she would try anything stupid, but she was a trained soldier. The heat level rose as they dipped beneath the surface, and he started to sweat. She wasn't the sweet, loving girl he'd once taken for granted, that was for certain. She was fundamentally changed, and yet she intrigued him even more. Whatever she claimed, there was still a bond between them, the tug of visceral attraction that no person from Neveks could ever deny.

When his mother returned, he would question her as to what exactly had happened all those years ago. He was no longer an idealistic twenty-year-old who'd been devastated at the evidence that his proposed mate hated his mother so much that she'd tried to kill her.

If he'd been thinking more clearly back then, he should've known such a claim was preposterous. At twenty he'd allowed his heart to rule his head, and allowed Rain to leave him, unchallenged.

"Your companion is in here."

Asar unlocked the door and motioned for the guard to stay outside as he followed Rain in. The strange human was sitting on the dirt floor, his back to the wall, his pale blue eyes fixed on Rain's face.

"Hey."

"Are you all right?" Rain rushed over and crouched in front of him, her expression so concerned that Asar concealed a growl.

"Sorry to be such an ass." The male cupped her chin and smiled into her eyes. "I was trying to make sure you were okay, and these guys caught me."

Asar stiffened as a blizzard of telepathic energy flowed between the couple at a speed that was barely decipherable and with a hint of something unworldly embedded within it. He couldn't decode it. That was *unheard* of for a Neveks male of his rank and telepathic power.

"*I* DIDN'T ASK *you to come here,*" Rain said quietly. "*After everything that has happened between us, I assumed you would be happy to see the back of me.*"

"*Why would you think that?*" Jay took Rain's hand and smiled at her. "*We're friends.*"

"*But I—*" Rain choked out her reply. After a wary glance back at Asar, who was frowning, she continued, "*I almost killed you.*"

"*Death by sex.*" Jay's tired grin warmed her in unexpected ways. "*What an amazing way to go.*"

"*I wasn't supposed to be able to do that,*" Rain hastened to clarify. "*The Queen Goddess said I was of impure blood and that I would never achieve full citizenship or be able to bond with my own kind.*"

"*But I'm not your own kind,*" Jay pointed out.

Rain stared at him. "*Maybe that's why it worked.*"

"*The big guy behind you is giving off all kinds of angry vibes. He's the Queen's heir, right?*"

"*No, Asar is her only son, but he can't be her heir.*"

"*Power passes through the female line?*"

Rain nodded.

"*Then who is the Queen's heir?*"

"*I'm not sure. She has an extended lifespan like the Oracle.*" Rain grimaced. "*She's probably disposed of all potential rivals.*"

"*You do not like her?*"

"*She banished me and lied to Asar as to why she did it.*"

"*Why would she do that?*" Jay held her gaze.

"*Because I once thought he was…*" She couldn't continue that thought.

"*He still is.*" Jay glanced over at the huge warrior behind her. "*I can sense his interest in you right now.*"

Rain shrugged. "*That's probably because he can't read our conversation, and that's never happened to him before.*"

"*Yeah, I'm getting that.*" Jay settled back against the wall. "*I'm not sure what your plans are, but I'm in no shape to leave yet. There's something weird going on with my bio data and A.I.*"

"*I know.*" Rain allowed herself a small smile. "*It contacted me.*"

Jay stared at her, his pale blue gaze pointed. "*Shit.*"

"Why can't I access your communications?" Asar strode closer and glared down at Rain.

"Because you're an ass?" she answered sweetly.

"It is not right," Asar said as Rain rose to her feet.

"Get used to it."

"It is something you both learned in the military?"

"Might be." Rain looked down at Jay, and her heart stuttered. He looked drained, and it was all her fault. Surviving an encounter with a mating Neveks female wasn't always a given for a Neveks male, let alone a human being. "We need to get him up to the healing center."

"Why?" Asar studied Jay as well.

"Look at him. He's obviously ill." Rain glared at Asar. "Do you want a friend of the Oracle's to die on your watch?"

"Of course not." Asar nodded slowly. "I will take him."

Despite his colossal failure to stand up for her with his mother, Asar had never been mean-spirited or lacking intelligence. Rain would give him that.

"Okay."

To her surprise, Asar bent down and swept Jay up in his arms. He'd definitely filled out his lanky frame in the last ten years and was now a massive muscled bulk of potent male.

"Tell the guard to open the gate."

Asar went up the many flights of stairs and strode through the healing center. He laid Jay down in the room next to Rain's mother's.

"Thank you," Rain said.

"You are welcome." Asar stood back as one of the healers fussed around Jay. *"You are not just his friend, are you?"*

Surprised by his sudden shift into telepathic mode, Rain had no time to block him.

"You've fucked him, haven't you?"

Rain stared back at him, daring him to start on her, almost hoping he would so she could erase her last memories of the young boy who'd loved her so passionately and promised to bond with her forever.

"That is none of your concern."

He glared down at her. *"Why do you think I live alone, Rain?"*

She raised an eyebrow. *"How would I even know or care that you did?"*

"Because since you left I have never sought out another mate."

Rain just about stopped her mouth from falling open. *"Why not?"*

"You know why." His amber gaze intensified. *"Your loss devastated me."*

"But you did nothing to stop it at the time."

"I was young, I believed the Goddess Queen was always right. I was trained to believe that." He took a quick breath. *"Why didn't you fight back and wait for my return?"*

"*Oh, it's my fault now, is it?*" She squared up to him, hands on hips.

"*That's not what I meant!*"

"I was also trained to believe that the Queen Goddess was always right, so when she told me I could never have a Neveks mate, what else was I supposed to do, Asar? Hang around and tell you that we could never be *together*? Watch you turn your back on me in disgust?"

Rain only realized she was yelling out loud when she noticed the horrified expression on the priestess's face, and that Jay was struggling to sit up. The healer took the opportunity to make a quick exit.

Asar took a step back and bowed to Rain, his expression icy. "Perhaps we should continue this conversation at a later date and in private?"

"Nope. I think I've said everything I need to say to you." Rain glanced over at Jay. "Sorry you had to hear that."

He shrugged and lay back on his pillows. "No worries. It certainly explains a lot."

"What do you mean?" Asar rounded on Jay.

"As in, there are a lot of telepathic undercurrents in this room, and now I think I understand them better."

"Even though you have had sex with Rain, they still have nothing to do with you, human," Asar snarled.

Jay looked at Rain. "You told him about that?"

"He guessed."

"Because he's still connected to you. Got it."

"He is *not*—" Rain almost raised her voice again, but gave it up in defeat as both men stared at her. "By the way, I can fuck whoever I like, okay?"

They both frowned, their offended expressions so similar that she blinked. "Now, just hold on a minute—"

Asar bowed. "Perhaps you should attend to your 'friend.' I will see you at dinner." He stalked off, slamming the door behind him so hard it rattled in its frame.

"I think you pissed him off," Jay observed.

"Good." Rain turned back to the bed. "Now, how about you lie down and let the priestess help you heal while I go and sit with my mother?"

JAY SLOWLY SHOOK HIS HEAD. "Seeing as we're alone, how about we discuss what happened the other night?"

Rain sighed and sat down on the edge of the bed. The blue silk of her dress slipped lower on her arm, exposing the soft curve of her breast. She looked like a different person in Neveks dress, which only made him want her even more.

"Do we *have* to?"

"Well, having sex with someone who morphed into some kind of fire-breathing dragon and almost threw me through a wall was something of a first for me," Jay admitted.

"I didn't think I was capable of bonding."

Jay studied her downturned face. "So that's how everyone from Neveks has sex?"

"No. Just those who are...mated. It is not something that is discussed much before a triad is formed."

A thrill of pure male satisfaction shot through him. "So we're mated?"

"*No!* We can't be, you're not from Neveks, and I'm..." Rain paused, and then groaned. "I don't know why it happened. I don't understand it at all. I'm just glad I didn't accidentally kill you."

"As I mentioned before, I'm hard to kill." Jay rubbed his neck where her fangs had pierced his skin. "Did you actually drink my blood like a vampire?"

"A what?"

"A mythical blood-drinking race who are scared of sunlight."

Jay registered her look of total confusion. "Obviously not a part of Pavlovian folk lore."

"I didn't drink your blood. I just—" Rain waved her hand around in a helpless gesture. "I just felt compelled to mark you like that."

"As your own?" Jay waited until she looked at him. He saw fear in her eyes. "I'm okay with that, you know."

"Jay…"

"I never thought I'd find a woman who could take my enhanced strength. You can." He hesitated. "You *owned* me."

She reached for his hand. "Jay, I'm not here to make alliances or find…mates or anything like that. I'm here to be with my mother until she dies. When the Queen returns, she will probably kill me anyway."

He sat up straight. "Not on my watch."

"You have no idea what she is like." Rain shivered. "She is so powerful she can sense your thoughts from hundreds of miles away and crush you with the power of her mind."

"But if we're mated, then we can fight her together."

Rain's shoulders slumped. "It won't make any difference, Jay. And I don't want your death on my conscience."

"My life and death are on me," Jay reminded her. "You can't tell me what to do."

"I can ask Asar to kick you out," Rain said, her chin in the air. "I'm sure he'd be delighted to do that for me."

"Not if I tell him we're mated." Jay paused. "But he knows that, right?"

She looked away. "He knows we've had sex. He probably doesn't think I can bond, so he wouldn't be concerned about that."

"So his mother is the Queen Goddess, and she's the one who kicked you out?" For the first time Jay wondered whether Asar was more involved with his mother's politics than he wanted to be, or whether he was her partner and collaborator.

"Yes. She said the Gods had spoken to her, and that I was not of true Neveks blood, meaning I could never aspire to being part of a mated triad."

"That must have been devastating," Jay said quietly. He knew how it felt to be abandoned like that.

"Yeah. She said I needed to leave as quickly as possible, and the next thing I knew I was on the bus going to the city. I'd never been outside Quoxor province before, and I was terrified."

Jay squeezed her hand hard. "And where was lover boy during all this?"

"He was away with a hunting party. I don't think he knew what his mother had planned for me."

"Right." Jeez, he wanted to punch Asar in the face and keep going until the big man was on his knees, begging him to stop.

"I've thought about it a lot, and I really don't think he knew," Rain said reluctantly. "He's not that kind of guy. I kept expecting him to come after me, to pull the bus over, take me in his arms and ride back to Neveks." She tried to smile and it almost broke Jay's cold, cold heart. "I was pretty damn stupid back then. Ten years in the military has changed that, at least."

"You weren't stupid. If you believed he loved you, why wouldn't you think he'd come after you?" Jay pointed out. "I would have."

"Apparently, his mother told him I tried to murder her and that I ran away."

"And he *believed* her?"

"She is the Queen Goddess." Rain shrugged. "Why would he not?"

"Because he was supposed to love *you*." Jay stuck to his guns. "Because anyone who has shared even a fraction of your mind knows that you're as honest and straightforward as pure gold."

She bit her lip and studied him for a long moment. "Thank you for that."

"You're welcome." He brought her fingers to his mouth and

kissed them, aware that he wanted to do so much more, but reluctant to destroy the fragile truce he had spun between them. If Asar was involved with the Queen's plans Jay would enjoy bringing him down even more because of what he'd done to Rain.

"You need to rest." As if aware of his less-than-pure thoughts, Rain eased away from him. "The healers will take good care of you. I will be right next door with my mother if you need anything.'"

"Good to know."

Jay made no attempt to detain her as she left. He was in no shape to take on a morphed Neveks female, especially here in the heart of the Queen Goddess's temple. He needed time to think about everything he'd just discovered and work out what he needed to do next to ensure he and Rain survived. He also had a mission for the Pavlovan inner council to complete which might end in his death.

The Queen Goddess was up to something. Everyone outside Neveks agreed about that, but what exactly she was doing was his mission to discover and share with the council. Was her son a part of her schemes? Rain seemed to think not, and she knew him far too well for Jay's liking. He'd have to be on his guard against the male who already intrigued him far too much.

Jay groaned and lay back on his pillow. In order to do *any* of that he had to regain his strength and find out what the hell was going on with his A.I. He sensed he was changing again, but his analytics weren't talking to him. Had Rain affected him on every level—physically, mentally, and emotionally?

"AFFIRMATIVE." His. A.I. confirmed his suspicions.

After the original insertion of the A.I., Jay had ceased to feel much emotion. His concern for Rain and his savage desire to protect her from harm was as shocking to him as it would be to his commander and his telepathic peers. He was the cold fish, the logical brain, and the killing machine. Now all he cared about was saving Rain, and to hell with anything or anyone who dared to get in his way. Even his mission seemed secondary, and that wasn't good.

Jay's eyes started to close. It was a good thing that all communication with Kaiden had been cut off when he entered Neveks. His mission was in peril, and all because a morphing Neveks female had almost fucked him to death. He had a sneaking suspicion that his boss wouldn't be very happy with him right now at all...

7

―――――

ASAR STARED DOWN AT THE FACE OF THE SLEEPING MALE AND considered his options. It was still early in the morning. He'd prayed in the temple, attempted to communicate with his elusive mother, and checked that Rain and her mother were still sleeping.

And now here he was, contemplating the interloper, the human who had dared to have sex with his woman…

"She's not yours."

Asar blinked down at the still form. *"You are awake."*

"I heard you blundering down the hall about half an hour ago. What do you want?" Jay opened his strange blue eyes and stared right up at Asar without the slightest hint of fear and more than an edge of mockery.

"Be careful, human." Eager to avoid the intimacy of telepathy, Asar spoke aloud. "Your life is currently in my keeping."

"I thought you were just a lackey for your mother?"

"What does that mean?" Asar growled.

"She is the supreme power around here. You can't do anything without her permission."

"That is something of an exaggeration. In her absence, and

without the presence of a female heir, I stand in her stead and can wield her authority."

"Does that bother you?"

"What particular part?" Asar asked.

"That you can never rule by yourself." Jay eased a hand behind his head on the pillow like he had all the time in the world to chat.

"Why should it?' Asar frowned. "The Queen Goddess has ruled us for hundreds of generations. It is just how it is, and how it should be."

"So as much as you'd like to kill me, you can't do it." Jay's satisfied smile made Asar clench his jaw.

"When my mother returns, I will petition her for the right to battle you in single combat. Will that shut you up?"

"Why?" Jay sat up, and the covers fell away from his upper body, displaying the paleness of his skin. Asar noted that he might not have much bulk, but his muscles were well-defined.

"Because you have dishonored a woman of Neveks."

"Bullshit. One, Rain was banished when she was eighteen, so she is no longer a 'woman of Neveks,' and, two, if anyone gets to fight for her honor it should be her. She'd be glad to take you on." Jay looked Asar up and down. "And she'd probably beat you as well."

Asar flexed his biceps. "I doubt that. And women do not fight in single combat."

"Tell Rain that, and see what she says."

"You would make your woman fight for you?" Asar jeered.

"Make her?" Jay had the gall to laugh. "I'd be the one holding her back."

"You dishonor her with your words."

"Yeah? Like you can talk about honor." All the amusement died from Jay's face. "The man who let her walk away from everything she knew and everybody she loved without even a whimper."

"That is not true," Asar snarled. "I was told that Rain had attacked my mother in the holy temple. She had witnesses!"

"And you chose to believe them because basically you're a momma's boy?" Jay shook his head. "Please."

Asar grabbed Jay around the throat and hauled him to his feet. "I am no coward."

"Rain thought you'd come after her, you fucker," Jay said fiercely. "You let her down just because you were scared of your mother."

With a roar, Asar drew back his fist and aimed it at the other man's face, but Jay was too fast for him. Furious, Asar tried again, and this time managed to take his rival down onto the floor, pinning him to the ground. Within seconds, Jay somehow rolled away and was on his feet again.

Asar turned on him. "Now, who's the coward? Do you always run away?"

"I don't want to hurt you while I'm a guest in Neveks, so don't try and provoke me." Jay righted a stool and went to sit on the side of the bed.

"You are the one provoking me!" Asar roared. "You are the one who has dared to touch my female! You deserve to have every bone in your body broken in two for forcing yourself on her!"

"*Forcing her?*" Jay shot to his feet, his mouth a thin line, his eyes icy. "Hell, no. She was a willing participant in everything we did."

"I doubt your word!" Asar shouted.

A FLICKER of movement drew Jay's attention to the door behind Asar where Rain was now standing, hands on her hips, and her expression stormy.

"Ask her yourself." Jay nodded at Rain who marched into the room and went straight up to Asar.

"He doesn't need to ask me anything! I heard him!" She poked Asar in the chest. "For the record, I'm the one who came on to Jay, *okay*? So stick that in your pie hole and smoke it."

"My pie hole?" Asar frowned. "What new insult is *this*?"

Jay fought an insane urge to laugh. "I think she means pipe, but I'm sure you understood what she was trying to say."

Asar ignored him, his attention fixed on Rain who was wearing just a bra and panties with her long hair flowing over her shoulders. Lust stirred low in Jay's gut. He wanted to grab her and take her down onto his bed and…

"Why would you choose to have…sex with a man like this?"

Asar sounded genuinely bewildered, and for a second Jay felt almost sorry for him.

"Who else would I be having sex with?" Rain demanded. "*You?*"

"Yes!" Asar thundered. "If you have stayed here instead of—"

"Running away?" Rain finished his sentence for him. "Your mother's bodyguard didn't even allow me to say goodbye to my *own mother* before they shoved me out the door!" She swung around and pointed at Jay. "I like having sex with him, and you know what? When he feels up to it, I'll have sex with him again!"

"Really?" Jay asked.

Rain shot him an exasperated look. "Yes."

Asar took a threatening step forward, and Rain blocked his path. "If you want to fight someone about this, then fight me."

"I would *never* fight you," Asar said hoarsely.

"Why not?" Rain asked.

"Because you are…too precious to me."

Jay stared intently at Asar, his mind catching the sincerity of the big warrior's words even as Rain rolled her eyes.

"Don't treat me like a child. I am a trained soldier."

"And yet I would still never hurt you," Asar murmured, one hand coming to rest on Rain's bare shoulder.

Jay tensed as the shock of that touch resonated through Rain and into him. *What the hell was going on?*

Asar's gaze flew to Jay. "I can feel you both now." He frowned. "This makes no sense."

"Then perhaps you should keep your hands to yourself." Rain shrugged off his touch. "Have you finished threatening Jay now? I need to get back to my mother."

For the first time, Asar slowly smiled. "I have noticed that your Jay does not respond to threats well."

"Good." Rain glanced over at Jay. "Are you feeling okay?"

"Yes. Thanks for popping by."

"You lie. Your energy levels are still pathetic." She came over and bent to kiss his cheek, her long hair shielding her face. *"I will not allow him to bully or hurt you."*

"Right back at you," Jay murmured, furious at his own continuing weakness. *"And, by the way, I think you could take him anytime you wanted."*

She snorted. *"He's twice my size and a renowned warrior, but I'd certainly go down trying."*

"Maybe we'll have to double-team him."

"It might come to that." She sighed. *"But—"*

"You don't want to hurt him, either," Jay said. *"He's still connected to you, Rain. I can feel it."*

She nodded and slowly straightened up, not denying his words at all. "Try and rest, Jay. I will check in on you later."

He wanted to hold onto her so badly that he had to grip the side of the bed with both hands to stop from reaching out to her as she left. He cursed softly as he lay back on pillows, his small store of energy depleted.

A shadow loomed over him, and he groaned.

"While are you still here? Didn't you listen to what Rain

said? She'll be back to kick your ass if you start messing with me again."

The big man crouched down on his haunches beside the bed and considered Jay.

"You are confusing my senses."

"Apparently I do that a lot to people from your planet."

Jay shivered as Asar reached forward and ran his fingers down the side of his exposed arm, stopping at his wrist before encircling it.

"Your mind is at war." Jay blinked at the accuracy of Asar's statement and tried not to show any emotion as his companion continued. "You already have scars from the first change, and now you are fighting another battle." Asar frowned, and closed his eyes. "Yet I cannot see the way clearly for you—only that you are gradually becoming clearer to *me*."

The rough pad of his thumb caressed the softer skin of Jay's wrist. "Do you understand what I am telling you?"

"Not really." Jay tried to shrug. The last thing he needed was for the Queen's son to have full access to his innermost thoughts. Seeing as it was obvious where Asar's loyalties lay, it could be a disaster. Or could he use the male's obvious interest in him to gain access to the Goddess?

Jeez, he was such a cold, cold bastard sometimes…

Asar let out a long, slow breath. "I think I should leave you now."

"Fine by me," Jay replied.

"But I do not want to leave you," Asar sounded as puzzled as Jay felt. "I want—" He shook his head, stumbled to his feet, and left, shutting the door quietly behind him.

Jay's hand slid beneath the sheets to cup his thickening cock. Some part of him had wanted to throw back the covers and offer Asar something more useful to do with his mouth than just talking.

"Damn…" Jay whispered. Asar was right. He wouldn't need

to feign interest in the Neveks male. He was already interested. Things were really getting out of hand.

———

"THERE IS something I wish to tell you, daughter."

"What's that?" Rain settled her mother back on her pillows and sat on the side of the bed. After her encounter with the two male idiots next door, she'd had to try very hard to find her calm center and help Alaya start her day. There was some weird dynamic emerging between herself and the two males that she was pretending to ignore—the very idea of it made her head spin.

"It is about your father."

Rain tensed as her mother took her hand and tried to squeeze it with her sadly depleted strength.

"I wish I'd gotten to meet him," Rain said softly.

"He was a good man, but even he was unable to resist the Queen in the end." Alaya sighed.

"What do you mean?" Rain asked.

Alaya leaned closer, her faded hair brushing against Rain's cheek. "I loved him, but the Queen desired him and took him from me."

"Why?"

Her mother shrugged. "Because she wanted him."

"But that sucks," Rain said.

"I agree."

"I thought he died in a hunting accident just after you became pregnant?"

"That is what the Queen told everyone, but I know she lied." Alaya drew a shallow breath. "A few weeks before the hunt, he sought me out and begged me to take him back, saying the Queen had bewitched him. We continued to see each other in secret."

"I don't understand," Rain said slowly. "If you and he were formally bonded, how could she take him from you?"

"Because she can attempt to erase those bonds." Alaya sighed. "In your father's case, her power over him wasn't strong enough to keep him besotted with her. She would never forgive him for that."

"So you think she arranged for him to be *killed* rather than let him come back to you?" Rain whispered.

"She and I are of the same family. I was carrying his child, and she was jealous of the enduring bond between us."

Rain sat back. "The more I hear about the Queen Goddess, the more I want to meet her and challenge her to a fight."

"You would not prevail."

"It would still be worth it."

Rain considered Jay's offer to fight alongside her. If he regained his strength, she might take him up on it. Any stranger who entered Neveks without the Queen's express permission could be executed at will. If the Queen chose to mess with Jay, then neither of them would have anything to lose...

Gods, she wanted to go back into his room, climb into his bed, and just hold him. Had she done something to his very soul? Had their sexual encounter destroyed him? The desire to bond with him, to share his thoughts was almost unbearable.

"Have you seen Asar, daughter?"

"Yes. He hasn't changed much."

"The night you left, when the Queen Goddess claimed you had attempted to assassinate her, I found Asar here in the temple. He was praying at the altar, with tears streaming down his cheeks." Alaya paused. "I have never seen him in this part of the temple since."

Rain tried to picture Asar crying, and couldn't. But there was no need for her mother to lie to her when her death was so close.

"Do you think he still cares for me?" Rain asked the question even though she dreaded the answer.

"Well, he has never sought out another mate, and, after you left, he made sure I was safe from his mother's wrath here in the sanctuary of the inner temple." Alaya smiled. "He was also the one who insisted you were informed of my condition."

"Asar did that?" Rain was genuinely surprised. "That was… good of him."

"If he still loves you, Rain, then perhaps, when I am gone, he will petition the Queen anew and ask to bond with you again."

"That's a lovely thought, Mother."

"Do you no longer care for him, then?" Alaya hesitated. "I sense another presence in your mind. Have you perhaps met your other Neveks mate since you have returned?"

"Not quite." Rain smiled at her mother, who needed all the hope in the universe right now. "But things are definitely looking up."

"MESSAGE from the Queen Goddess for you, sir."

"Thank you." Asar nodded as he took the sealed envelope from the male courier. Why his mother couldn't simply send him a telepathic thought he wasn't sure, but sometimes she preferred this arcane way to communicate. She insisted it was more secure.

He opened the envelope and took out the single sheet of parchment.

Treat the human as a guest in our house. Do not allow him to leave and do not trust him.

Well, that was clear enough. He took the paper to the fireplace, tossed it into the fire, and watched it burn.

But why? Asar stared into the flickering flames as they curled around the blackening paper. Interlopers were usually removed from Neveks immediately. Did his mother know that Jay was connected to the Oracle's family? Even if she did, would that sway her from carrying out a heavy punishment? She disliked the Oracle at Quoxor immensely and had always been jealous of her superior reach and power over the majority of the planet's citizens.

In truth, Asar had begun to wonder whether her obsession with the Oracle had become unhealthy. When the Temple at Quoxor suffered an attack from the hostile planet of Etrusca, his mother had seemed disappointed that the Oracle and her daughter had survived. She had also refused to send help when a transport carrying Senator Ash had crashed nearby, insisting that the people of Neveks had no responsibility to assist an organization that oppressed them.

When the Queen Goddess returned, Asar would have to speak to her about many matters. Part of him was ashamed of his own compliance with her orders. Had she ruled for too long? Had her sense of fairness deserted her? But that was in the past. With Rain to fight for, and the intrusion of the human into the sacred Neveks Temple, things were changing. Perhaps it was past time to review the old way of doing things and finally hold his mother, goddess or not, accountable.

8

ASAR OPENED HIS EYES, AND STARED UP AT THE CEILING. HE'D woken from an erotic dream about the male Rain had brought with her to Neveks. The thin sheet that covered his body was now tented over the thickness of his heated erection. He slid a hand beneath the cover and grasped his cock firmly in one hand as he continued thinking about the scenario he'd previously been dreaming about.

His mouth on the human's cock, the human's on his…their minds locked together in lust.

Even as he stroked himself, he leisurely catalogued Jay's slim frame, the taut muscles in his arms and chest that spoke of a strength not as obvious as Asar's, but equally dangerous. And the human's *mind…*

Stop making me hard.

Jay's amused thought crashed into Asar's mind.

With a curse, Asar got out of bed, fashioned the silken sheet into a garment, and strode back along the hallways to the inner sanctum of the Temple. No one stopped his passage. In his mother's absence, he was the supreme authority in Neveks.

He went through into Jay's room. A single candle burned

near the side of the bed where Jay lay on his back, one hand grasping his cock while he pleasured himself.

With a groan, Asar crashed to his knees and glared at Jay.

"What spell have you cast upon me?"

"I've done nothing. You think I like this?" Jay demanded. "You think I *want* to wake up dreaming of your mouth on me, making me come?"

"*Shut up.*" Asar leaned in and simply closed his mouth over the crown of Jay's wet cock and swirled the taste around his tongue. His own shaft kicked up again with the sheer thrill as Jay gasped and thrust upward. But Asar refused to take more and concentrated his efforts on teasing and nipping the most sensitive parts of Jay's crown, his tongue dipping into the slit, his teeth grazing the heated, pulsing flesh.

A second later, pain shot through him as Jay shoved a hand through his long hair and yanked hard.

"*Take more.*"

Asar ignored him.

"*Am I too big for you? Are you afraid?*" Jay taunted as he attempted to force Asar's head back and away from his cock. "*Don't you want me thrusting deep down your throat making you gag and beg when I come?*"

With a last savage nip, Asar reared back and swallowed Jay's shaft whole from tip to root.

"*Jeezus...*" Jay gasped.

Asar sucked hard, sliding his mouth up and down Jay's shaft as the other man bucked and cursed under him. Jay's fingers loosened in Asar's hair, his grasp turning into a sensual, scratching caress on his skull.

Jay's other hand was busy, too, working its way down through the layer of silk knotted at Asar's waist to fondle his ass and stroke and play with the soft skin of his taint and puckered hole.

"*Touch my cock,*" Asar demanded, so glad that telepathy meant he didn't have to release his grip on Jay's cock to speak. He was mouth-fucking Jay hard now, enjoying the stiff presence crowding his throat and the ripples of sensation quivering through the heated column of flesh.

"Be my guest."

An image flashed into his head of Jay's mouth on him and Asar instantly complied, levering himself up onto the bed and presenting his needy cock. Even as he resettled himself over Jay, he fought the scream of pure delight when the other male took him deep and sucked him hard.

They moved together like seasoned lovers. Mouths locked around each other and minds in harmony as they silently fucked, neither of them willing to be the first to come.

Jay returned to probe Asar's ass, and he bucked hard as the tip of Jay's finger pushed inside him. It was enough to send him over the edge. Fighting the urge to bite down or roar his pleasure he came in long, shuddering waves down Jay's throat, triggering an answering rush of come from his companion.

For a long moment, Asar just lay still, waiting for his heart to stop pounding and for his breathing to return to normal, before he rolled off Jay and onto the floor.

"You're leaving?" Jay asked as he wiped his mouth, his fingers lingering and tasting in a way that made Asar's cock twitch again.

"I do not want this, and neither do you," Asar said as he restored order to his rumpled bed sheet. Even as he spoke, his gaze was hungrily roaming down Jay's naked form.

"It's just sex." Jay yawned.

Asar took a hasty step toward him. "It is more than that. You are in my head. *No one* can do that to a Neveks male."

"As I told you before, I'm different." Jay reached down and cupped his balls and cock, his thumb rubbing small circles that made Asar's mouth go dry with lust.

"This can't happen again," Asar said firmly.

"Hey, you're the one who came in here."

"Only because you don't know where I sleep."

Jay raised an eyebrow. "You don't think I could find you in a heartbeat if I wanted to?"

"You are a prisoner here on sufferance, so, no, you could not." Too late, Asar remembered his mother's order to treat the human as a valued guest.

"Trust me, I'd find you if I wanted you." Jay sat up, his pale eyes narrowing. "No one would be able to stop me."

Asar curled his lip. "Well, seeing as I will not be chasing you down again, you might have to prove that to me."

"Don't worry, if I'm overcome with lust and want that big, hard cock of yours again, I'll find you." Jay yawned again. "Biggest I've ever had, so thanks for that."

Asar went still. "You have bedded other men?"

Jay's smile died. "They don't break as easily as women."

"You like to hurt people when you have sex?"

"Not intentionally." Jay paused. "Unless that is something they crave, of course." He rose to his feet and squared off with Asar, who tensed. "Next time we do this, I want you on your knees sucking me off, your hands clasped behind your back so you can't touch yourself unless I order you to do so."

Asar opened his mouth to reply, but it was as if all the air in his lungs had been sucked out. The only response his body could muster was the swift and betraying hardening of his cock.

Jay's smug smile as he glanced downward made Asar yearn to hit him.

"Yeah. That."

Asar swung at him, but Jay caught his wrist in a surprisingly iron grip.

"Don't fight it. You know you'll do it."

"I have *never*—" Asar finally found his voice.

"I know you haven't, but you will." Jay rubbed his thumb over Asar's skin. "Maybe I'll yank your head back, and pull your hair really hard while you're sucking me, make you fight yourself to keep me in your mouth."

Asar's breath hissed out as he imagined the scenario. He shook off Jay's grip and strode toward the door. The sound of the other man's laughter followed him out into the hallway before he carefully closed the door. He only managed a few steps before he had to slow down and lean against the wall. His cock was hard again, his thoughts in chaos.

What were the Gods playing at? Sending him this heathen human who seemed to understand him in a way no other person ever had before? How did Jay know the secret fantasies he'd harbored since he'd become a man? Fantasies that as the Queen's son he'd had to hide because in his position he had to be seen as the strongest man in the kingdom?

His knees buckled. He slid down to the floor, and stared unseeingly at the wall opposite him. He wanted to go back, wanted everything that Jay had just offered him…

"Asar? Are you all right?"

He went still as Rain's concerned voice came from his left. Gods, not now. Not when he was feeling so weak and confused.

"Go back to bed," Asar ordered her.

"Don't tell me what to do."

"Go!" Asar roared.

"You condescending idiot!" She came closer and kicked him hard in the shin.

With a roar he sprang to his feet and reached for her, bringing her to the floor beneath him even as she hit and fought him all the way down. It took far longer than he had anticipated to immobilize her beneath him, and he was breathing hard by the time he managed it.

"Let me up, you big stupid oaf!"

Her green eyes flashed in warning, and her skin tone changed to a fiery red.

In reply he shoved his knee between her thighs, lowered

himself down and settled his aching cock against her stomach. He had both her wrists clasped between one of his hands above her head.

He went to kiss her, and she bit his lip, which made him want her even more.

"Kiss me, Rain."

"In your dreams," Rain scoffed, but there was little she could do to get away from him, and her body and mind were enjoying the physical contact way too much to want to relinquish it just yet. His cock was hard against her, and all that was female in her was yearning toward him and softening.

"Kiss me."

"Fuck you," Rain snapped.

"Even better," Asar licked the seam of her lips, and she stiffened.

"Where exactly have you just been?" she asked him out loud.

He focused on her, his golden gaze perplexed. *"What?"*

She bit his lip hard, and he recoiled and reared up over her, which gave her just enough time and space to kick him in the stomach and roll away. Unfortunately, she'd missed his balls, but he was still groaning, which was immensely satisfying. But she wasn't done yet.

She marched to Jay's room and went through the door. The faint smell of come and sweat told her everything she needed to know.

"Rain." Jay was sitting up in bed, his gaze watchful and alert. "What's up?"

She pointed behind her. "Did you fuck him?"

"Why would you think that?"

"He tastes of you." Her words came out as more of a snarl. "And you're *mine*."

"What is it with you Neveks that you insist on trying to own everyone?" Jay asked. "Asar is as bad as you are."

The door behind her closed, and she became aware of Asar moving closer.

"You fucked him," Rain repeated.

"We fucked each other's mouths, so what?" Jay shrugged. "You're not the only one who is allowed to fuck who they want."

She growled low in her throat, and the tips of her fingers itched as the beast inside her asserted its ownership and attempted to unfurl its claws.

"Rain…" Jay's eyes widened. "Fuck, no. I'm sorry. Don't do that."

Like she could stop herself or even wanted to. He was hers, she had tasted his blood, mated with him, and—

Asar grabbed her arm and spun her around. "Rain—what the Gods is going on? You are acting as if this male is yours."

"He is MINE," Rain growled.

Her claws extended more fully, and Asar's breath hissed out as they dug into his skin.

"What in the Gods name is wrong with you?"

She hissed a warning and shoved him hard in the chest, sending him flying backward to sit down beside her traitorous mate.

"I should kill you both." Her words barely made sense as her heat level rose, and her fangs pricked the roof of her mouth.

Both men were staring at her now, their gazes narrowed and filled with a strange mixture of fear and anticipation. Her inner self loved that. Loved the thought of biting and ripping and tearing into them—

"Daughter…be still. Come to me."

With her last coherent thought, Rain forced herself to breathe deeply as her mother's voice resonated urgently in her mind. This was *wrong*. She refused to become a monster. She had to control herself, force her mating self back within her skin, and then get the hell away from the two men who were currently driving her insane with lust.

She thought of her mother and of the candles in the temple, pictured the beauty of the altar, and the Goddess within. Her claws retracted, and her jawbone eased back. With a soft cry, she turned on her heel and ran toward the sanctuary of her mother's room.

JAY'S BREATH shuddered out of him and he caught hold of Asar's tunic.

"Let her go. She'll be safer without seeing us."

"What in Gods' name was going on?" Asar breathed. "I have never seen a female from Neveks act in that way."

Jay gave Asar a quick look, but the man didn't appear to be lying. Was it possible that an unmated Neveks male had no idea what a female transitioned into when she mated and bonded? Asar's mother was hardly an average woman, so it was possible that he had no concept of how narrowly he and Jay had just avoided being mauled by a furious, rutting female...

"She obviously believes she has some...interest in both of us," Jay said carefully. "Which I suppose makes sense, seeing as I've had some kind of sex with both of you."

Asar groaned and lay back on the bed. "This cannot be happening. I am the Queen's son. Rain is a banished Neveks female, and you... *You* aren't even from this *planet!*"

"You can ignore it all you want," Jay said. "But let me tell you that you're not the only one with a problem."

He'd been sent to Neveks to investigate the Queen Goddess and had ended up getting sexually involved with her son and the woman she had banished. His boss was going to kill him if the Queen didn't manage it first.

Jay threw himself back on the bed beside Asar and stared glumly up at the ceiling.

"Dude. We're screwed."

"Daughter."

Rain ran to her mother and threw herself into her arms.

"*Help me.* Help me control this," she whispered. "I don't know what to do."

Alaya kissed the top of her head. "The Queen told me that because your father wasn't one hundred percent Neveks you weren't a full-blooded female, and that I should not mourn your loss because you would never breed or mate anyway." She sighed. "Just another thing she lied to me about."

"I didn't think I could do it either," Rain confessed. "And then one night, just before we arrived here, I...morphed and almost killed my companion."

"The human prisoner?" Alaya shuddered. "I am surprised you did not."

"He isn't like most men." Rain hesitated. "He doesn't break easily."

"Obviously." Alaya chuckled. "If he survived, he is probably your true mate."

"But then there is Asar..."

"Who has always been bonded to you." Alaya paused. "Why are you sad? Most females would be ecstatic to discover both their males in the same place. Your sexual bond will be outstanding."

"Did you have another mate?" Rain asked.

"For a little while." Alaya smiled. "There was a delegation from Hakron. Your father and I met our third—he was acting as an interpreter. His mother was Neveks and his father had a Hakron grandfather. His skin color was quite confusing. That's why when the Queen said you weren't pure Neveks I wondered whether our third was your father, but when you were born you looked all Neveks to me."

"Maybe that's why I could bond with the human," Rain said slowly. "Maybe the Queen is wrong, and we can look beyond the borders of our lands for mates."

"No one has ever said we can't mate with others. The Queen has always wanted to preserve the uniqueness of our telepathic abilities."

"By making us feared and disliked by the rest of the population, and by denying people the right to find their mates and form triads." Rain reminded her. "How can that be *good* for us?"

"The Queen cannot know what you have done, Rain." Alaya gripped her hand hard.

"How can she not know when her son is one of my supposed mates?" Rain groaned. "She's going to kill me anyway, but I don't want to bring Asar and Jay down with me."

"If they are truly bonded to you, they will not let you face her alone."

"Then I will have to try and meet with her privately," Rain said. "I refuse to allow her to kill anyone other than me."

Alaya kissed her cheek. "Then may I suggest we consider ways to keep you from morphing? There are techniques that have been developed to help a female control her impulses. If you had remained with me, I would've taught them to you as a matter of course. But it is never too late to begin."

Rain managed to smile and took a deep breath. "I hope you can teach me fast. I don't think the Queen Goddess will take long to come back if she realizes I have a thing going on with her son and an outsider, do you?"

There was a knock on the door, and the healer appeared. "Are you feeling well enough for a visitor, Princess?"

Alaya released Rain's hand and sank back onto her pillows. "As long as it isn't the Queen I can manage a few minutes."

Rain scowled as Jay and Asar came in through the door. She pointed her finger at them. "Don't upset my mother, okay?"

Both men came in and dropped to their knees beside the bed. Asar reached for Alaya's hand and kissed it, then Jay did the same.

"Greetings, Princess," Asar said softly. "I am sorry to disturb your rest, but I wished to make the foreigner, Jay, known to you."

Alaya smiled at them both and then turned slightly toward Jay. "Gods greetings to you, Jay. My daughter has told me a lot about you."

Rain felt like squirming as heat rushed through her.

"It is a pleasure to meet you, my lady," Jay said. "Your daughter is a very special female."

Asar almost growled and attempted to turn it into a cough, which made Rain want to laugh, which was totally inappropriate.

"She speaks highly of you, Jay." Alaya paused to gather her breath. "I am glad to have met you. I know you will do everything in your power to assist her to continue in good health."

Rain began to protest, but Jay talked over her. "Princess, I swear that I will always protect her from harm. Not that she needs me to do that, but I am more than willing to oblige."

"Thank you." Alaya turned to Asar, her expression grave. "Despite your exalted position, I expect the same from you."

The conflict on Asar's face was plainly visible to Rain. "I will never hurt your daughter. I can at least promise you that."

Rain tried not to snort, but couldn't deny the sincerity behind Asar's quietly spoken words. He'd try to help her, but if it came down to it, would he really defend her if his mother told him differently?

"You doubt me."

"With good reason," Rain replied to his thought.

"I will not let my mother kill you."

She blinked at him. *"And how will you keep your word if she orders you to do just that?"*

"I will not let her kill you." He placed his hand over his heart. *"Believe that at least."*

Rain didn't bother replying to him. Her silence should tell him everything he needed to know.

Jay rose to his feet. "We should leave."

"Yes, my mother needs to rest." Rain stood as well. Asar bowed and headed for the exit, pausing to greet the healer as he left.

Rain followed Jay to the door, and he caught hold of her hand. "Do you have a moment to talk to me?"

Rain gave him her best frown. She really didn't need another lecture about her current abominable behavior. "About what?"

"It's important."

"I'll just settle my mother, and I'll be right over."

Her mother was already half asleep, so she was able to liaise with Jay quite quickly. She shut the door behind her and waited. "Well, what is it?"

He was pacing the room, his expression remote and his gaze icy. For the first time she saw the technology that controlled him rather than the man.

"Which is safer here, our telepathic link or just talking?" Jay demanded.

She frowned at him. "Why?"

"Just tell me."

"Talking probably, although we seem to have developed some kind of special link that no one else can penetrate." She paused. "What's up?"

He came close and met her gaze. "Which will make you believe me more?"

She tapped her skill. "This, obviously. It's harder to lie."

"Your mother is getting weaker."

"I'm aware of that." Ray stiffened.

"Who prepares her food and drink?"

"The priestess, why?"

"Don't lose your shit." Jay took her hand in a firm grip. *"But I think your mother is being poisoned."*

RAIN'S green eyes flashed with shock, and she stumbled backward.

"What in Gods' name are you talking about?"

Jay refused to let go of her hand. *"As soon as I got close to her, my A.I. sent out an alert and began to analyze her breath. Someone is trying to kill her, Rain."*

"But why?" Rain shook her head. *"She's not on the council, and she's not in the Queen's favor."*

Jay hesitated. While he'd been waiting for her, his A.I. had done thousands of computations for likely scenarios and had come up with two possibilities—neither of which he liked, but both of which he was going to have to run by Rain. He switched to speech in case he inadvertently gave away too much information.

"The two highest probabilities are these. One, that the Queen has a reason to dispose of your mother that we are not aware of, or, two, the Queen wanted a reason to get you back here, and deliberately made your mother ill enough to warrant an excuse for your return."

Rain frowned. "I don't like either of those options."

"Neither do I," Jay agreed. There was a third more torturous possibility that involved him, but he wasn't going to share that one just yet. There was no reason to muddy the waters when all Rain currently cared about was what was going on with her mother. "Is there any way you can get me a sample of her food and drink so I can analyze it properly?"

"That will be simple enough. I'm the one who sits with her

and makes sure she eats." Rain paused. "I suppose the Queen could say *I'm* the one poisoning my mother. That would be just her style, and, considering my reputation as a potential assassin, the general population would probably agree with her."

She was taking things very calmly, but he wasn't surprised. She was a strong woman.

"We have to keep this from Asar," Jay said.

"That shouldn't be hard. He can't access our link."

"Yet."

Rain glared at him. "You think he's part of our Triad, too? My mother does."

Jay stared at her. "Shit, I hadn't even thought of it like that. What if he is?"

"Don't play dumb." She poked him in the chest. "You're the one who's been...fooling around with him."

"Trust me, I didn't want it to happen."

"So you're telling me he *forced* you to suck him off?"

Jay fought a smile. "Not exactly. I can't explain what happened. I don't think either of us likes it, but there it is. We're both with you now."

"Then we can't have full sex with him," Rain said firmly.

The image of that exploded in Jay's mind, and he swallowed hard.

"No." Rain glared at him. "He is the Queen's son. If she is poisoning my mother, then he's either aware of it, or he's going to have to pick a side, and that's not fair on him or us."

"If he is mated to us, hasn't he already chosen?" Jay asked.

"We haven't had real sex with him."

"You mean the kind when you morph and try and fuck us to death?"

She glared at him. "*Yes.*"

"God, now that you've mentioned it, I'd love to see you own his ass the way you owned mine."

"Stop it." Rain's skin flashed red, and she shivered. "You're not helping."

"Because you'd love to do that to both of us."

"We were talking about my mother. Can we stay on topic?" Rain asked.

"Sure." Jay shoved his erotic dreams aside and focused on practicalities, which was supposed to be his strength. "Get me those samples, and we'll take it from there."

Rain left, and Jay sat down on the bed. With everything that was going down, he really needed to talk to Kaiden and get some idea whether the Queen was powerful enough to have anticipated his arrival and made plans to bring him and Rain down. Or was it even worse? Had someone on the high council revealed their plans to the Queen?

Neither scenario made him happy. He trusted his fellow soldiers, and Kaiden was gold. The only other member of the council who knew everything was Ash, and Jay would swear on his soul that he wasn't a traitor. Ash's Second Male had been injured during a clash with the Etruscans, and Ash himself had almost been assassinated on a deliberately downed plane.

So, either another member of the council was taking information from Ash, or the Queen Goddess really did have the power to infiltrate even the most secure of networks…

Jay rose from the bed and went to find where Asar had his quarters. The guard at his door had mysteriously disappeared the previous day and had not been replaced. Having already established a link with Asar—whether he liked it or not—Jay had no problem finding his way.

He knocked and went straight in to find Asar sitting at a table. He appeared to be eating and drinking so Jay sat opposite him and helped himself.

"What do you want?" Asar growled. "Haven't you tormented me enough for one day?"

"Firstly, where's my guard gone?"

"My mother said you are free to move around the temple, but that you cannot leave the city until she returns."

"She's coming back?"

"So I understand."

"When?"

"Soon." Asar glared at him. "It is not my place to question the Queen Goddess."

"So I gathered. She basically gets away with doing what the hell she likes, doesn't she?"

"She listens to my counsel."

"*Right.*"

Asar visibly released a long, calming breath. "Do not start arguing with me again."

"Why not?" Jay asked. "Are you afraid that you'll leap on me, and we'll end up fucking?"

"Yes."

Jay sat back. "Well, that's honest."

"If you have finished, perhaps you could leave?"

"I haven't finished." Jay met Asar's gaze. "If I have to stay here until the Queen returns, I need to send a message to my friends in the Temple of Quoxor to say I've been delayed so that they won't worry about me."

"You cannot communicate with them telepathically?"

"Between this Temple and that one? Apparently not." Jay wasn't sure if that was true, but he sure as hell wasn't going to try and get a vitally secret message out through a society that had no telepathic filters. "Can I just write them a note and get you to deliver it?"

Asar regarded him for a long moment as he sipped from his goblet. He'd replaced his silk tunic with something more substantial that covered his chest and thighs. His long, dark hair was tied back in a neat braid. Jay preferred him naked, but that wasn't going to happen.

"Do you have to ask your mother if that's okay?" Jay asked.

"No. I am merely considering your request."

"It's not exactly hard." Jay tried to look innocent, and then remembered Asar was already under his skin and roaming around his head. He focused on his shields.

Asar stood and Jay automatically stiffened, but the big man did nothing more threatening than fetch pen and paper from a desk in the corner of the room.

"You may write your message. I will make certain it is delivered at all speed."

"Unless you'll let me go there myself and then come back." Jay took the writing implements and spread them out on the table.

"That's not possible, and you know it," Asar said flatly. "Write your letter I will read it and then I will seal it in front of you."

Asar was not going to let him move from the spot, which made sense. He obviously didn't want Jay doing anything funky.

Jay clicked on the pen and considered what to say. He needed to alert O'Neill to the possibility that the plan had been discovered, and he needed to do it a way that wouldn't make Asar suspicious.

O'Neill, I'm held up in Neveks territory helping out an old military friend of ours, Rain Datta, so don't worry that I haven't arrived yet. As your favorite Scottish poet would say: The best laid schemes o' mice an' men, gang aft agley. Jay.

He passed the note to Asar who read it through, a frown creasing his brow.

"What does the last line mean?"

Jay shrugged. "It means things don't always go to plan. O'Neill comes from Scotland, so he'll get the joke."

"I see." Asar read the note again, and then just stared at it before reaching for the sealing wax and a candle. "I'll have it sent out today."

"Thanks." Jay finished his bread and rose to his feet. "If I'm free to move around, can I train with you?" He gave Asar's body an approving glance. "I'm sure you do something to keep so fit."

Asar's skin flashed gold and red. "I train with the Queen's guard every day. You are more than welcome to join us."

"Great." Jay nodded. "Just let me know when."

He walked out, confident than Asar would send the note and that O'Neill, who was as sharp as Jay, would get the message that things might be cocked up and relay that information to Kaiden. At least he damn well hoped so.

9

"I CAN SYNTHEZISE AN ANTIDOTE TO NEUTRALISE THE POISION."

"Okay." Jay nodded. *"How will we get that into the patient?"*

"DISSOLVED IN WATER. IF SHE CONSUMES A SUFFICIENT QUANTITY BEFORE SHE INGESTS SOLIDS SHE WILL NO LONGER SUFFER SYMPTOMS."

"That sounds remarkably easy. What do I need to get for you to create the antidote?"

His A.I. ran a list of ingredients past him.

"Can I get those here?"

"AFFIRMATIVE. ALL AVAILABLE WITHIN 5 METERS OF YOUR CURRENT LOCATION."

"In the temple?"

"YES." A map flashed in his head.

Jay considered his options. He'd probably have to enlist Rain's help and maybe even the healer who looked after him. She'd probably have access to all the remedies in the temple stillroom, which was where his A.I. was directing him.

The sooner he got the antidote made, the quicker Rain's mother would recover. He wasn't sure if she would ever regain her full health, but he could certainly stop her dying right in front of her daughter. If they managed to "liberate" Neveks from the claustrophobic power of the current Queen Goddess, he might insist she was treated in the capital city.

He walked across the hallway to where Rain was sitting with her mother. Through the half-open door he could hear them talking to each other, the sounds affectionate and full of laughter. He'd never had that in his life. Once his mother had died, no one else in his family had wanted anything to do with him. Things had only gotten worse when the government had become afraid of their own creations and tried to exterminate him and his companions.

Some of that had been his fault. He'd grown used to being powerful and had pushed the boundaries to their limits—he'd almost taken out an entire tank crew with the cold-blooded ferocity of an assassin. He understood the lure of power all too well now and was no longer prepared to sit back and allow the Queen to ruin more lives in her quest to rule the planet.

Rain and her mother deserved to be together. He'd do anything in his power to make that happen.

"Jay?"

As if sensing the promise in his thoughts, Rain turned toward the door where he stood. He beckoned for her to come to him rather than disturbing her mother. Today she wore a simple green tunic belted at the waist and her hair was tied at the nape of her neck. Her skin seemed to redden as she approached him, and all the hairs on his arms came to attention.

She smelled of flowers and incense, and he wanted to pick her up, take her to his bed, and devour every inch of her...

She gave him the eye. "*Concentrate.*"

"*I can do two things at once you know,*" he protested.

"*Not if you are doing them properly. Now what can I help you with?*"

He had to remind himself that beneath this new softer exterior version of Rain, there was still a warrior with a very decisive mind and an ability to cut through his crap.

"I need a reason to visit the stillroom to gather some ingredients."

"Then I will take you there."

Jay frowned. *"Won't that make people suspicious?"*

"Only if you act like an idiot."

She disappeared out of the door and came back with the priestess who was currently looking after both Jay and her mother.

"Marz will keep an eye on my mother while we take the tour of the temple I promised you."

Jay bowed to the priestess. "Thank you."

"You are welcome." Marz smiled at him. "I am pleased to see that your own recovery is proceeding as planned."

"I feel much better thanks to your generous care."

They went out into the hallway where a soft breeze wafted through the ancient stone pillars, reminding him of the church he had attended as a child with his mother. Whatever his own personal feelings about the Gods, he couldn't deny that some spaces were definitely infused with power.

"This way." Rain took a right turn and he followed her.

"You seem very familiar with this place," Jay commented.

"I grew up here in a house in the temple grounds."

"Not in the actual temple?"

She gave him a sideways glance. "My mother worked here."

"It's very beautiful."

"Yeah, and didn't prepare me for the outside world at all. It's bad enough for the average Neveks person who goes outside the boundaries, but for me it was…eye opening."

"Yet you survived and thrived."

"We are both survivors in our own ways, Jay."

He stopped walking to look down at her, his heart beating way too fast.

"Don't compare my stupid, reckless life with yours."

She raised an eyebrow. "Why not? I've been in your head. I *know* you."

"That I've *killed* and maimed and—"

She pressed her fingers to his lips. "So have I. It's okay. I understand."

He stared at her for a long moment, and she gazed into his eyes with a wry warmth that made him want to drop to his knees and howl like a banshee.

"What is a banshee?" Rain asked.

"A spirit who wails and warns of forthcoming death."

"Very fitting then." Her smile disappeared. "We are both survivors, Jay. The real question is whether we can survive what's coming next."

"The Queen?" He grimaced. "Yeah. That's a tricky one."

She grabbed hold of his wrist. "But I will resist her. She doesn't deserve to rule this place."

"Then I will be at your side." She began to speak, but he kept going. "That is not negotiable. We fight the Queen together, and we die together."

"That's hardly encouraging."

"It's not meant to be." He paused. "But if we can get Asar on our side and bond him to us…"

"Even that might not be enough. My mother said that the Queen can sometimes break the bonds between mated triads."

"Wow," Jay breathed. "Then we really are screwed."

Rain's smile held a hint of desperation. "Let's just see if we can help my mother and forget about the rest."

Jay started walking again. "Agreed. You distract the priestess while I gather the necessary ingredients. Asar will have to wait."

HIDDEN behind one of the pillars, Asar stayed where he was until Jay and Rain reached the end of the corridor and entered the stillroom. He had no idea why they wanted to go there, but that was the least of his concerns right now.

He let out a long shuddering breath. He hadn't heard all of their conversation and hadn't consciously sought to spy on them. But he'd heard enough to understand that Jay posed a threat to his mother, and that Rain was in agreement with him. He pressed his palm over his heart, which felt as if it was actually hurting. They thought they could persuade him to become their ally. They would use his unwilling attraction to them to force his hand.

Asar groaned softly and stared at the wall opposite. The trouble was, he *did* feel a connection with Rain and Jay. It consumed him. What if they were his given mates and he had to kill them to protect his mother?

He closed his eyes and sent a telepathic command to his mother. *"You must speak to me. What do you know of this human who has invaded the sacred sanctuary of Neveks?"*

"He is dangerous. He is using his unnatural powers to convince Rain that she is bonded to him and that she has a true grievance against me." Asar tried to relax as his mother responded.

"Then why don't I just send him on his way to the Temple at Quoxor?" Asar demanded.

"Because I wish to meet him."

"But what if he persuades Rain to attempt to kill you?"

His mother laughed. *"You have such little faith in me, my son. I am more than a match for Rain Datta."*

"But I don't want you to hurt her." Asar held his breath as the silence lengthened.

"If you can contain your lust for a few more hours, I will be with you. If she is foolish enough to challenge me, I will attempt to spare her life. What you do with her after that, is up to you."

Asar stiffened at the cold indifference in his mother's voice. Had she always been like that? Had he chosen to ignore this side of her power because it hadn't impacted him so personally before? If that was the truth, he was ashamed of himself.

"Listen to me, my son. The human is dangerous. He is a machine designed by his government to kill without remorse, and is in league with the Etruscans. He will do anything to achieve his purpose including manufacturing false feelings in Rain to make her feel wanted and loved. If you wish to help her, perhaps you will make her aware of this."

Asar's hands fisted. *"Then I will send the human on his way to Quoxor and speak to Rain."*

"NO! I forbid it. I wish to see this abomination in person."

Asar winced as a bolt of pain lashed through his mind. His mother never liked being disobeyed or challenged. Despite the threat, he tried again.

"But your decision makes no sense. Why not remove the threat?"

"Because I wish to see him suffer! How dare this male think he can assassinate me by using one of my own people? I WILL NOT STAND FOR IT!"

She slammed the link shut with a brutality that sent Asar to his knees, blood dripping from his eyes and nose as her rage screamed through his head.

It took him a few moments to gather himself and stumble back to his quarters. The last thing he needed was for Jay and Rain to find him passed out in the hallway. He slammed the door shut and locked it, gulping down the fresh air.

His mother was…acting like a paranoid monster. His childhood sweetheart was plotting with another man to kill the Queen Goddess, while he was being treated like a pawn by all of them. Anger simmered in his gut as he contemplated his choices. Whatever he chose, someone was not going to be happy, but this was not the time to shirk his responsibilities. These were not trivial matters. His choices would affect the state of Neveks for generations to come.

He would talk to Rain. She was his priority. He would not allow his mother to ruin her life once again.

Jay handed Rain the powder. "Just add this to your mother's water and make sure she drinks a cup of water before every meal."

"That sounds simple enough." Rain dealt with the full jug and then touched Jay's shoulder. "Thank you."

He shrugged. "Thank my A.I."

"YOU ARE WELCOME."

The thought reverberated through both their heads, making Rain jump. She kept her hand on Jay's shoulder, enjoying the warmth and flexibility of his skin as she breathed him in.

"*Rain...*" Jay's voice stirred in her head.

She snatched her hand away and stepped back. They were still in her mother's bedroom.

"You should go."

Jay nodded and went to the door.

Rain fixed a smile on her face and walked toward her mother. "Everything okay?"

"Not really." Alaya met her gaze. "What's going on?"

Rain hadn't discussed what she intended to tell her mother with Jay, and he hadn't asked her to keep it a secret. Rain sat on the side of the bed, leaned in, and spoke rapidly under her breath. "Jay thinks you are being poisoned. He's developed an antidote, which I'm going to add to your water. That means you can continue to eat normally and not stir up any suspicions, okay?"

Alaya stared at her for a long moment and then slowly nodded. "I understand. I will be careful."

The fact that her mother didn't even question her made Rain

even more convinced that Jay was correct. Her rage at the Queen Goddess multiplied tenfold. When she saw that bitch…

Alaya took her hand. "When you are in her Temple, cover your wrath, my love. She will sense it."

"I don't care. I want her to come after me," Rain snarled.

"She will. I have no doubt of that now. Do you?"

RAIN LEFT her mother and walked briskly down the corridor toward the gardens. She had no real idea where she wanted to go, but she needed to work off her rage somehow.

"May I walk with you?"

Asar was coming down the steps toward her. Ah, perfect.

"I am not in the mood for company right now." Rain barely managed to be civil.

He hesitated on the bottom step, towering over her, his skin glowing like a waning sunset. He carried his sword and helmet in his hand as if he was just off to train with the palace guards.

"I would not normally press my case, but it is essential that I speak to you," Asar said quietly.

"Let me guess." Rain put her hands on her hips. "You've talked to your god-awful mother, and she's told you she's going to kill me so you've come to tell me your promises mean nothing. Guess what? I never believed you anyway."

"You are wrong."

"About what?" Rain snarled. "The fact that you'll cave and let her do whatever the hell she wants to me, or that she owns you?"

His mouth set in a firm line. "This is not helpful."

"It's helping me," Rain was shouting now, and she didn't care who the hell could hear her. "I'm sick of the whole lot of you! Especially you!"

"But I only wish to help."

"*Right*, and how do you propose doing that? Killing me nicely before your mother rips me limb from limb from the inside out?"

"Here's a suggestion." He came toward her. "I propose you stop listening to that human!"

"He makes a lot more sense than you do."

"Rain, he isn't what you think," Asar said urgently, taking her hand. "He doesn't have your best interests at heart."

"Says who?"

"My mother. She believes he is an assassin sent by the Etruscans to kill her." Rain attempted to pull out of his grasp. "No, *listen* to me! I know you hate her, but she is as outraged as I am about a human attempting to exploit a Neveks female."

"Bullcrap," Rain snapped.

"No! She sent me information on your human. He was designed as a weapon, as an assassin. He *has* no emotions, Rain. He would kill his own mother and almost did just because he can!"

He pushed the information into her brain telepathically. "At least read what she sent me. I ask only that."

"Get out of my head!" Rain shoved Asar hard in the chest and his eyes flashed red. "I *know* Jay—"

"No, you've fucked him, and he's used your loneliness against you." Asar held up his hands.

Rain shook her head, her whole body trembling. "You have no idea what you are talking about. I *know* him."

"You know *nothing*!" Asar was as angry as she was now. "He will use you to kill the Queen, and then walk away without a qualm to find his next victim. He *has no soul!*"

"And you are delusional." Rain met his gaze. "I actually feel sorry for you. Go back to your damned mother and tell her it didn't work. Tell her that Jay doesn't need to make me want to kill her. I want to do that all by myself."

"I don't want you to die." Asar spoke so quietly that Rain almost didn't hear him.

"So?"

"I heard you talking to Jay. He said he would use me against my mother if he could." Asar paused. "Don't you think he'll use you as well, Rain? Ask him why he is really here in Neveks and see how honest he is then."

With a sharp nod, he turned on his heel and left her alone.

Rain continued walking, replaying the conversation in her head and answering every point he made in a better and more scathing way until she stopped to sit down on a bench beside a fountain.

Jay had told her that he was an emotionless killer. She'd seen that side of him. He was obviously enhanced physically because he'd survived his first night mating with her. Nothing Asar had told her was a surprise up until that point.

But was there anything else? She considered the information Asar had placed in her mind. Should she look at it? Would that be a betrayal of Jay? Was it possible that a man who was suggesting that they bind the Queen's son to them more closely might also be willing to take on a Neveks female, and bet that his enhancements would help him survive the night?

He was probably the only man alive—who wasn't a full-blooded Neveks—who could make that calculation. Rain stared at the water pouring in the fountain as she dredged up her memories of the beginning of their strange relationship. He'd told her he knew nothing about Neveks or her culture...

She slowly raised her head. What if he'd lied about that? He had abilities far beyond her own and she sometimes sensed he was still keeping things from her... What if he'd lied about everything since they'd first met?

10

ASAR KNOCKED ON JAY'S DOOR AND THEN THUMPED IT SO HARD with his fist that the door gave in and opened voluntarily. For once, Jay wasn't in bed but was sitting by the fire, his expression so remote Asar almost didn't recognize him.

"What's up?" Jay looked over at him.

"I wanted to warn you."

"About what?" Jay asked.

Asar came in and shut the door behind him. "My mother will be returning to Neveks in the next day or so."

"So what?"

"My suggestion is that you leave this place and go to your friends at Quoxor."

Jay raised an eyebrow. "But you told me that no one could leave Neveks without the Queen Goddess's approval. Is this a direct message from her?"

"No." Asar folded his arms over his chest. "It is all my idea."

"Do you think I would leave Rain to face your mother alone?"

"I have received assurances from my mother that she will not kill Rain."

Jay stood and faced him. "There are many ways to take away a person's will to live. I'm sure your mother is a woman of her word, but please allow me leave to doubt her sincerity in this matter."

"What about yours?" Asar demanded.

"My what?"

"Your sincerity. Why exactly are you here, Jay?" Asar asked. "What power did you use to entrap Rain and bend her to your will?"

"Entrap Rain?" Unbelievably, Jay smiled. "Dude, you have no idea, do you?"

"You are not what you seem, human. Why not accept this opportunity to get away that I offer you?"

Jay angled his head to one side. "Why are you so anxious to get rid of me? Do you think Rain will suddenly fall into your arms and be just like her old self if I disappear? She is a different person, my friend. There is nothing either of us can do to change that—and thank the Gods for it."

"I can protect Rain," Asar said.

"From your own mother?" Jay half-smiled. "I suppose you might be the only person she would listen to. If you can protect Rain, what about me?"

"You don't need protecting. You are the problem here. Why did you come to Neveks, Jay?"

"I told you. To make sure Rain was safe."

"She is safe. I will make sure of that, so you can be on your way."

"You want me to leave?" Jay asked.

Asar forced himself to nod. "You are a complication that I do not require in my life."

"A complication?" Jay's blue eyes flashed ice. "I'm a lot more than that, buddy."

Asar met the glare head-on. "Oh, that's right. I'm a conduit to my mother. Now why would that matter to you, Jay?" He looked for something in the other man's expression, some discomfort, a flicker of shame, but there was nothing. His heart twisted. What had he expected from a machine? "You don't give a damn about me or Rain, do you? All you want is a route to my mother."

A second later, he was on his back on the floor with Jay on top of him, one hand wrapped around his throat in an unshakeable grip that tightened with every second.

"You'll send me away?" Jay growled. *"You'll deny this fucking bond that neither of us want between us? You're a goddammned coward."*

"I'm a realist. You're faking this and you know it! Now get off me!"

"Faking this?" Jay leaned in and ground his mouth against Asar's in a rough kiss that made Asar's heart stutter before Jay lowered his head to bite his throat. *"Read my fucking mind, Asar! Tell me that I'm not going to fuck you blind in the next five minutes whether you're ready for me or not!"*

Asar groaned as a flood of salacious images took over his mind, making his cock hard and his heart beat fast enough to burst.

"This is not helpful."

Jay glared at him. *"If you're going to kick me out, then I'm going to have you at least once so you know what you're missing, what you're throwing away."*

He slid a hand between them, grabbed Asar's already erect cock, and yanked on it hard before sliding down and settling his mouth over the crown, swallowing him whole.

Asar's mind shattered into a thousand pieces as he desperately tried to push Jay away. He stiffened as Jay nipped the side of his cock and instead pushed his hips up in a desperate attempt to offer Jay more.

Jay was not kind. He was not merciful. He took Asar to the very edge of sanity, making him claw at the air and then at Jay, who refused to slow the pace even when Asar came in hot, juddering waves down his throat. Giving him no respite, he started to suck him again, and Asar's cock responded until he was hard again.

WHAT THE HELL was he doing? Jay sat back, gasping, and stared down at Asar before slowly wiping a shaking hand over his mouth. He tasted Asar's come, blood, and sweat, and his own cock twitched. The red rage filling his mind slowly receded and he rolled away. If this was how Rain felt when she mated, he was amazed she could stay sane. God, he wanted to flip the male over, and fuck him blind...and then make Asar beg for more.

Jay fought for sanity, clinging onto the comforting background noise of his A.I., seeking the remoteness and lack of emotion he'd taken for granted for the last ten years. Asar didn't deserve to be treated like this. No one did.

"I'm sorry." Jay cleared his throat. "I was out of line."

Asar rolled onto his side, and then up onto one elbow, one hand now cradling his cock and balls. He looked magnificent, his long hair around his shoulders, his kaleidoscope skin spiraling with colors like the spinning of the universe.

"Why are you stopping?"

Jay turned away from the alluring sight. He'd lost his temper when Asar had suggested he meant nothing to him. He hadn't done that for years. Between Rain and the Neveks male, he was truly screwed. He had no right to be angry because Asar was correct. He *had* come to Neveks with an ulterior motive.

He just hadn't expected to find the only two people on the planet he wanted to fuck and protect for the rest of his life.

Wearily, he shoved a hand through his short hair. "As I said, I was out of line."

"So you'll leave?"

"I can't do that, Asar." Jay hesitated. "I've made promises I can't break." If the other male searched his mind, he'd hopefully realize that Jay was speaking the truth. "I can't leave Rain, and I don't want to go."

"But you planned to bind me to you more closely. I heard you plotting with Rain." Asar slowly got to his feet; the silk that had been wrapped around his waist fell to the ground in a sensuous rush, leaving him naked.

Jay closed his eyes against the luscious sight, and leaned back against the wall. "Yeah."

"Then why aren't you finishing what you started?"

"Because…" Jay set his jaw and forced himself to meet Asar's suspicious stare. "I'm a fool. I didn't mean for any of this to happen, Asar. I swear it on my mother's grave."

"The mother you tried to kill after your government removed your soul?" Asar hunkered down in front of him, and Jay tensed.

"Who told you that?"

"*My* mother."

Jay held his gaze. "After I was… enhanced, I was on leave. One night I got drunk and smashed up a local bar. The police brought me home, and I was still fucking furious. I pushed her out of the way when she opened the door."

"I didn't realize my own strength." He grimaced. "She fell and broke her collarbone. I didn't know she had severe osteoporosis. She never really recovered." He made himself look up. "I have to live with that for the rest of my life."

Even as he explained, his mind was spinning like trapped vermin. How the hell had the Queen Goddess gotten hold of that piece of information? That file was supposed to be buried so deep in his military records that even a planetary excavator couldn't find it. A wave of cold dread enveloped him. If the Queen knew about that, she probably knew about the plan to extract information from her willingly or not. Maybe he should leave…but how could he do that if Rain remained? And she would stay. She wanted her own vengeance. He knew that in his soul.

Jay forced himself to concentrate on the man in front of him. From his shocked reaction it seemed that Asar had no prior knowledge of what the Queen had found out. Perhaps there was a way to salvage something. If he could take Rain to safety at Quoxor, he could come back and face the Queen Goddess alone.

He bowed his head. "Thank you for your warning. If Rain will leave with me, I will go."

Asar's smile was pained. "We both know that she will not leave."

"Then I'm sorry, but you're going to be stuck with me as well."

There was a hint of pity in Asar's gaze that made Jay tense. "Maybe you should ask her about that first. She might prefer it if you leave."

"Why? What have you done?" Jay asked slowly.

"I warned you both." Asar shrugged. "She now has the same information that you do."

"About my past?"

Asar nodded as Jay got to his feet. "You are not the only one who feels as if their loyalty is being put to the test."

"I get that. You aren't in a great position, are you?"

Asar grimaced. "My mother is my Queen and the Goddess on earth. How can I disobey her?" He thumped his chest. "But my heart is at war with my head. The thought of Rain—or of you—dying at her hands appalls me."

Jay cupped the other man's rigid jaw. "I'm sorry for turning up and fucking with your life."

Asar moved his head until his lips brushed against Jay's palm. "The fucking I can take. The disruption of everything I once held true is…more difficult, but maybe I have been wrong. Maybe I too need to reassess my relationships."

He bit gently down on Jay's thumb. "Your mouth on my

cock, your hands on me..." He shuddered. "I want that more than I want to breathe." He hesitated. "Will you stay and fuck me just once before you go and seek out Rain, and perhaps change everything forever?"

"Won't that just make things worse?" Jay murmured.

"Worse than imagining what I might have had for the rest of my life?" Asar asked.

"But what if your mother orders you to kill me?"

Asar's desperate laugh was laced with need. "I could not do that to you *now*, let alone after you have fucked me." He wrapped one arm around Jay's hips, bringing their bodies into alignment. "Please."

Jay stepped back so that he could see up into Asar's face. "If we do this, you must know something important. I do it because I want *you*, not because I want you on my side. But if your mother tries to kill Rain, I will defend her against anyone, including you, with my life."

"I understand." Asar slowly nodded his head and gestured toward his bed. "Our time together is for us."

ASAR SAT on the side of his bed and waited to see what Jay would do next. The struggle was evident on the other male's face. If Jay walked away from him now, Asar would regret it for the rest of his life.

Without speaking, Jay came toward him, tearing off his shirt to reveal his muscled torso and the scars of a true warrior. He stepped out of his pants and was as naked at Asar, his cock already hard and wet.

"The colors on your skin," Asar said. "They do not move."

"My tattoos?" Jay glanced down at his bicep. "They are black and blue, and stay very boring."

Asar licked his lips as Jay moved to stand between his

spread thighs. Jay gently pushed him back onto the bed before straddling him. He braced himself, but Jay did nothing but slide his hands over Asar's torso, pausing to pinch his nipples and test the strength of his upper arms. Their cocks were aligned and rubbed against each other with every move Jay made.

Asar moaned deep in his throat. Jay leaned in to kiss him, wrapping one capable hand around both their cocks and gripping them hard. Pre-come spilled out, making Jay's job easier and slicker.

"You are so fucking beautiful," Jay murmured. "I could watch your skin all night."

"I'd rather you fucked me," Asar said. "This interlude will not last long."

A wave of sadness crossed Jay's face. "Yeah. I know. This is just for us before I go face the wrath of Rain." He nipped Asar's shoulder. "Stop being so practical."

"I—" Asar gasped as Jay shifted his grip and slid his fingers lower to tangle with Asar's balls and stroke his taint. "That is good. That is—" He arched his back, offering more as Jay's slick finger rimmed the hole of his ass. "Gods…"

Jay urged him backward until his head was on the pillow and his feet planted squarely on the mattress, his thighs spread as wide as they would go. Asar felt exposed, his need, his huge erection blatantly obvious, but he didn't care. He wanted Jay to take everything, and there was no shame in that.

Jay held Asar's balls and cock in one cupped hand, fondling him while he used the fingers of his other hand to play with Asar's ass.

"Lube?" Jay asked.

"In the drawer." Asar gestured to his right.

"You've done this before?" Jay asked as he found the glass pot and unscrewed the lid.

"Only with myself," Asar admitted.

"Yeah?" Jay came down for a quick savage kiss. "I'd like to see that."

Asar almost climaxed at the very thought of being watched.

"You've been with women, though?"

"Not since Rain."

Jay went still and stared down at him. "That's surprising."

Asar shrugged. "After she left there was no one who tempted me."

"Until now."

"Yes." Asar held his breath as Jay's lubed finger eased inside him. "That is…good."

"Mmm…" Jay moved position and knelt between Asar's thighs. "Let's make it better." He took Asar's cock in his mouth and thrust his finger deep, making Asar groan aloud. It was heaven. It was hell. He didn't know what to do with himself, whether to shake and moan, or come, or…

"Don't come until I tell you to."

Jay's telepathic command entered his mind, and he clung to the order, forcing his body to accept what was being done to him and just enjoy it. Just when he thought he could endure no more, Jay released his cock and sat back.

"Get on your knees and put both hands on the headboard."

Asar awkwardly complied, aware that a single brush of the covers on his stimulated cock might mean disaster. He faced the wall and then bowed his head, his long hair trailing onto the bed as Jay pushed his thighs farther apart, making his back arch, offering himself to his conqueror.

Jay bit his shoulder, and Asar shuddered. "Please."

"You want me?"

"Gods, *yes.*"

"Then have all of me."

Asar bit his lip, drawing blood as Jay thrust forward with his cock and took his ass. He breathed out hard, accepting the thick length inside him.

"*THAT'S BETTER.*" Jay gathered Asar's hair in one fist like the reins of a beast, jerking his head back. "*I don't have time to be gentle with you. I don't want to be. If this is our only chance I want you to remember me. I want your ass still sore when you have to face your goddam mother. I want my come in you.*"

Asar just moaned. Jay eased his hips back, and then shoved his whole cock deep, making the other male shudder as he took the brunt of the thrust. He did it again and again, root-to-tip, taking Asar into a rough, frenzied place of need Jay had never experienced with another man before.

Their minds joined, sharing the experience in a new way that was so powerful and intimate that Jay almost recoiled from the raw beauty of Asar's need.

"*I need...to...come. Let me come,*" Asar begged.

"*Not yet.*"

Jay thrust harder, his motions becoming ragged as his own need to climax fought his desire to stay exactly where he was forever. He reached around to grab Asar's hot, wet cock and yanked on him hard. With a shuddering groan, Jay let go, filling Asar with his come as their minds fused together in an unbreakable bond. This male was no traitor. He was far more honorable than Jay would ever be. Asar climaxed, and his hot seed was forced through the grip of Jay's fingers.

Jay set his teeth on Asar's throat, scraping the exposed flesh, feeling the other man shudder beneath him. He didn't want to move. He wanted to stay locked both physically and telepathically to the other male forever. Whatever happened next, he would not regret this meeting of minds and regaining the ability to feel.

With one last, lingering kiss, he moved away. "I wish you well, Asar."

His companion turned onto his side and looked back at him, the remnants of passion receding behind his royal dignity.

"And I you, Jay."

Jay gathered his clothes but didn't attempt to put them on. He'd walk back to his room and bathe in the temple pools before setting out to speak to Rain. Asar wasn't aware of it yet, but if Rain truly chose to fight him, Jay might not survive to meet Asar's mother after all...

11

Rain's head throbbed, but whether it was due to the approaching thunderstorm or the tumult of her emotions she wasn't quite sure. The fact that her mother would probably live after all was still too astounding to contemplate. She'd stayed in the Temple gardens, reluctant to take her bad mood back to her mother and unable to shake the horrible suspicion that Jay, the man she had bonded with in the most complete way possible, had deceived her.

It was getting dark, and the lamps surrounding the Temple had been lit, sending long shadows stretching over the elaborate gardens. The heavy scent of night-blooming flowers advanced and receded on the breeze flowing down from the mountains. It was very quiet, as if everything and everyone was holding its breath.

Rain raised her head. The Queen was coming. She could sense the disturbance in the air.

"Rain?"

She jumped as a figure stepped out of the gloom to face her.

"Jay."

She didn't get up from her seat, but waited for him to

approach her. He'd bathed, but the scent of Asar clung to him both physically and telepathically.

"You fucked the Queen's son." Rain didn't make it a question.

"Yes." Jay halted in front of her, his expression resolute, like a soldier about to go into battle or get his ass handed to him by a superior.

"Even though he is your enemy, and will do whatever his mother tells him to."

"Yes." He shrugged. "I don't think he could kill either of us."

"So you fucked him to keep him on your side?" Heat uncoiled in her gut along with devastation. Hadn't she learned never to trust anyone? "Just like you did to me?"

"I fucked both of you despite myself, and contrary to every order I have been given."

"Right. Poor old you." She slowly rose to her feet. "I'd ask you how you can live with yourself, but that would be pointless, wouldn't it? Asar was right. You have no soul. When did you decide to use me to get into Neveks?"

He set his jaw and stood at attention, as if determined to take anything she threw at him.

"From the beginning."

Any hope that she'd harbored about his innocence died instantly.

"I was ordered to meet you at the terminal and find a way to accompany you to Neveks."

"By fucking me?"

"No!" His blue eyes blazed fire. "I was supposed to get as close to Neveks as I could and then knock you out and pretend you were injured so they'd let me in with you. After I got into the city, I was on my own."

"Why should I believe a word you are saying?"

"Because why the hell would I lie to you right now?" Jay snapped. "The Queen is coming. She's going to try and kill us both. The best thing for you to do in my opinion is leave so that I can complete my mission."

"Me, *leave?*"

"Yes, and take Asar with you."

"So you can do what exactly?" Rain asked.

"Talk to the Queen face to face."

"*Talk* to her?" Rain shook her head. "I don't believe you, and I still don't understand what the hell you're doing here."

His mouth firmed. "I can't tell you that."

"Of course you can't. You've lied to me the whole time, haven't you, so why should you tell me the truth now?"

"Because I can't betray my superiors."

"But you can betray me and Asar, the fools who let themselves be fucked over by a soulless *machine*."

He visibly flinched. "If that's how you think about me, okay, but I swear that none of this was supposed to happen." His mouth twisted. "I didn't know we would…*bond* like that. I had no idea—"

"Stop right there." Rain held up her hand. "You're pretending you didn't do something to trigger that response in me?"

"What the hell is that supposed to mean?" Jay demanded.

"I'm not supposed to be able to form a Neveks mating bond."

He took a hasty step forward. "So you'd rather believe the Queen who ran you out of town than the male who gave up his fucking blood and ran out of *come* for you?" His face twisted. "You fucking nearly killed me. Do you think I expected *that?*"

She was trembling so hard now that she was surprised he hadn't noticed. "Why not, when you're probably the only male on this planet who would survive such an encounter?"

He looked like she'd slapped him. "You think they sent me *deliberately?* That I *knew?*"

Rain raised an eyebrow, trying desperately to remain cool while her whole world collapsed around her. "Of course I do."

He stared at her for a long moment, his gaze unfocused. "If

they did, I knew nothing about it." His smile contained no humor. "Not that you will believe me anyway."

"Why don't *you* just leave and let me deal with the Queen," Rain suggested even though her heart was breaking into pieces.

"I can't do that."

"Why not? You want her dead, and I want her dead. She'll be gone anyway."

"I need to speak to her."

"Right…"

"I can't explain why, but I can't let you kill her before I talk to her."

"You don't understand what you are dealing with. I'll barely have a second to strike her. She is all-knowing. If I pause to let you have your little chat, she'll take us both out with a thought."

Jay visibly collected himself. "Then maybe it is still in our best interests to work together."

Rain opened her mouth to blast him, and he carried on talking. "Just hear me out. I know you don't trust me, but we do have this mating bond between us. Won't that help us withstand the Queen's power?"

Reluctant to admit that Jay might have a point, Rain considered him in silence for a moment before asking, "How do I know that you won't just use me as a shield while you attempt to keep the bitch alive, and that when you're done with her, you'll let her take me out?"

His expression darkened. "Because I could *never* do that. You are my mate!"

The fact that she wanted to believe him so badly stiffened her resolve, and she stepped back from him.

"I'd rather take my chances alone, thanks." She turned on her heel. "The Queen is coming. You'd better work out exactly what you are going to do before she screws with your head. Good luck. Thanks for nothing."

"Rain…"

She walked away from him because it was the only thing left to do. The Queen would probably kill her, but she'd make sure she got a few good blows in before she died. Jay and Asar would probably meet the same fate if they decided to intervene, which meant any stupid fantasy she'd harbored about the three of them living in a bonded triad was dead on arrival. She had her pride—Jay had shredded everything else. There was nothing else to do but depend on herself and follow through to the end.

"*Rain,*" He came up behind her and grabbed her arm. "Don't do this."

She snarled at him as a red mist clouded her vision. "Let go of me."

He tightened his grip. "We need each other. Come *on*, work with me here."

She leaned into him until he started to relax, and then sank her teeth into his throat. "*Don't mess with me right now, or I'll rip out your larynx.*"

Even as he froze to attention, the scent of his skin and his blood made her fingers curl into claws with the need to throw him to the ground and fuck his brains out.

"I'm okay with that," Jay breathed.

She shoved him away from her, for once her strength equal to his. "I don't have time to deal with you. I have the Queen to face."

"Then face her with *me*. Let me help you."

"You are not my problem."

"So you won't support your bonded mate?" Jay asked.

"You deceived me. You did *something* to me to make this happen! Once you've gone, I bet I won't be able to bond with a rock!"

"You'll be dead. We'll all be dead."

She held his gaze. "Then maybe that is our fate, and we should just accept it."

"Bullshit. Stop being so goddamned heroic!" Jay snapped. "I'm going to talk to Asar."

"Good, maybe you can fake-bond with him as well," Rain said sweetly.

The look he shot her as he marched away was murderous enough to make Rain's knees tremble, but she knew she was doing the right thing.

The Queen was coming. There was no more time.

Gathering her courage, Rain walked back up the stairs to the inner temple and went into her mother's bedroom. Her mother was already looking more alert and was sitting in her chair rather than propped up in bed.

"The Queen has sent a message commanding us to meet her in her chambers."

Rain's heart thumped double time. "Both of us?"

"Yes." Alaya held up her hand. "And don't think you can talk me out of going. I intend to be with you until the end."

"That's not very comforting." Rain grimaced as she sat opposite her mother.

"I've been thinking about why she tried to poison me," Alaya said.

"We don't know it was actually her," Rain observed.

"Don't be silly, my darling. Nothing happens in the temple without her agreement." Her mother shifted in her seat. "There was a prophecy that disturbed her greatly."

"About what?"

Alaya pursed her lips in thought. "About a triad that would rule all others, and bind the nations together."

"What's that got to do with what's happening now?" Rain demanded.

"After she recorded that prophecy, her attitude toward us changed. We were no longer valued relatives, but enemies. She made sure I ended up sequestered in the temple and you... Well, we all know what she did to you and how she excused it."

"I still don't get what you mean," Rain said gently. "I'm not important enough to merit a prophecy let alone one that would make the Queen banish me."

"Then why else did she make you leave? What was she afraid of?"

"She also allowed me to return to tend to you," Rain reminded her mother.

"Because she needed a reason to make you return, and by poisoning me to near death she found one."

Rain's hand slid to the dagger she'd "borrowed" from Asar, concealed within her flowing skirts. "The only way we will get any answers to these questions is to go meet with her."

"And probably die before we get the chance to ask a thing."

Rain scowled at her mother. "You're not helping."

Alaya shrugged as she rose to her feet. "I have lived a good long life. I am not afraid to face my maker. If fate decrees it is my time to depart this world I will go willingly."

"Good for you." Rain took her mother's hand, and tucked it into the crook of her arm. "I'm not quite so ready to die just yet."

As Rain and her mother approached, the doors into the Queen's private apartments swung open to reveal the Queen sitting on her golden throne with Asar at her side. The sight of him made Rain falter. He looked stern, his arms folded over his massive chest and his long hair tamed in a severe braid.

"Queen Goddess." Alaya bowed. "Welcome home."

Rain didn't bow, but stared instead at the ornately tiled floor, raising her telepathic shields as high as they would go.

"Thank you." The Queen smiled. Despite her great age, she was a beautiful woman with skin containing hints of metallic elements rare among the people of Neveks. Her eyes were almost black, and her hair was long and streaked with silver. Power emanated from her in unsubtle waves. Rain had always found the Queen terrifying, and was dismayed to realize that at first glance, nothing had changed. She reminded herself of everything the Queen had done to her family and stiffened her resolve.

"Rain."

"Yes, Queen Goddess?"

"Do you not wish to thank me for allowing you into Neveks to attend to your mother?"

"It was very gracious of you." Rain dared to raise her gaze. "As you can see, my mother is looking much better."

"I had noticed that." The Queen's power enveloped the room, making Rain shiver. "A miracle indeed."

"As soon as my mother is fully recovered, I promise I will be on my way," Rain added. "As long as she remains in good health, you will never need to see me again."

"How kind of you." The Queen paused. "Unfortunately, you will not be leaving for quite some time. There is the small matter of you bringing an Etruscan assassin into my realm to be dealt with first."

"I don't know what you are talking about," Rain countered. "I was captured alone as I approached the gates of Neveks. You can ask your security forces. That's the last thing I remember."

Asar came to stand beside her. "Rain is correct, my Queen. The error in bringing the human into Neveks was all mine."

Rain could barely stop herself from gazing incredulously up at Asar. He hadn't needed to step in and defend her. He was risking his future for nothing.

The Queen's smile didn't falter. "You were duped by the pair of them, my son. I cannot hold you responsible."

"You don't need to." Asar straightened up. "I take that blame willingly, and I cannot agree that the human is an Etruscan spy."

Rain swayed against Asar as a wave of telepathic annoyance swept through her mind and desperately focused on her shields.

"You know nothing, my son." The Queen's voice was chilly now.

"As your chief security adviser I would hope that isn't true." Asar raised his eyebrows. "Are you suggesting you have kept vital information about the security of our land from me?"

"I am the Queen Goddess, no one questions me or my power."

"I understand." Asar bowed his head. "But I still stand by my original view. Now that Lady Alaya has recovered, why not let Rain and the human continue their journey on to Quoxor?"

"And reveal secrets of our sacred sites to the Oracle and her family?" The Queen's voice rose with each word. She was definitely not used to being crossed by her own son.

"I would never do that," Rain said.

"You have been compromised by a charlatan. Your opinion is suspect," the Queen snapped.

Rain considered the distance between the Queen's chair and her current position. If she moved now would she be able to reach the Queen before Asar stopped her?

"*NEGATIVE.*"

Jay's A.I. boomed a response in her head, and the Queen stiffened.

"What was that?"

Rain hastily tried to block the A.I.

"I'm not sure," Asar said slowly.

Rain tried hard not to look guilty. If Asar could hear the A.I. as well, it meant the three of them were even more deeply connected than she had realized.

The Queen turned to one of her guards. "Bring the human to me."

"His name is Jay," Rain spoke up. While the guard left the

room, she edged closer to the Queen. "He is a soldier originally from Earth."

"I know who he is."

Asar also spoke. "He is a friend of the Oracle's daughter and her First Male. They have already contacted me and intimated that if he does not arrive safely at the temple in Quoxor, they will be speaking to the senate of Pavlovan."

The Queen snapped her fingers. "That bunch of worthless politicians. What can they do to challenge the power of Neveks? Nothing!"

"We cannot stand alone, Mother," Asar said quietly. "We depend on trade agreements with the other regions and with the cities."

"Then we need to find other ways to overcome that dependence."

Rain caught her mother's worried gaze. The fact that the Queen was openly discussing policy in front of them did not bode well for their future survival.

She took another wary step forward. "Might my mother return to her room now? She is becoming weary."

The Queen stared at Rain for far too long before abruptly nodding her head. "Yes. She may leave."

Alaya took Rain's hand. "I would rather stay here with my daughter."

"And I insist that you leave." The Queen raised her chin.

"Not until I have your solemn vow that you will not kill her."

Rain suppressed a gasp at her mother's bravery and desperately squeezed her hand.

"I will not kill her," the Queen said reluctantly. "Now, please withdraw from my chambers."

Rain turned to her mother and kissed her cheek. "Please go, Mother. Remember that I love you with all my heart, and that will never change."

Alaya's smile was beautiful. "Do what you must, daughter. I will support you."

With one last lingering glance over her shoulder, Alaya left the chamber. Rain couldn't decide if she was relieved or devastated that her mother would not have to watch her attack the Queen. If she failed, which was likely, her mother would probably suffer as a result, but she seemed at peace with that.

As Alaya reached the door it was opened from the outside by the guard to allow her to pass through. While the guard was distracted, Rain eased her dagger from under her skirts, and leapt for the Queen. As everyone shouted around her the Queen reacted with a mighty telepathic swipe that sent Rain to the ground screaming in pain, her weapon falling from her hand.

Asar picked her up from the floor and held her tight, one broad arm across her chest restricting her breathing even more as blood poured from her nose and ears.

"See my son? See the viper that has come amongst us again?" the Queen cried. "I *told* you she was an assassin!"

Rain struggled to get out of Asar's grip. "You deserve it, you bitch! You had my father murdered! You've been poisoning my mother! What the hell is *wrong* with you?"

Asar cleared his throat. "I know none of this. Is she speaking the truth?"

The Queen rose to her full height. "She just tried to kill your mother, and you are questioning and accusing *me*?"

"I know Rain. She would only pursue this vengeance if she thought it justified," Asar said firmly

"Then let me go and let me finish this!" Rain kicked him hard in the shins, but he refused to budge. She summoned Jay's A.I. "*Help me out here.*"

"*HELP IS ON ITS WAY.*"

Even as the A.I. responded to her, the door opened. Jay came in and walked straight up to the Queen. Asar hastily deposited Rain on the floor and barred Jay's path.

The Queen didn't move from her chair, her expression furious.

"Where are your guards?"

Jay shrugged. "I disposed of them on the way." He glanced over at Asar and Rain. "Glad to see you are both still alive."

"My mother has sworn not to kill Rain," Asar said.

"She's already bleeding and hurting," Jay snarled. "That is unacceptable."

"She tried to kill me like the good little assassin's pet she has become." The Queen smiled. "If you do not surrender immediately, I will take her mind and leave her alive, but a drooling wreck for both of you to fuck as you will."

"Mother—"

"Be quiet, you fool!" the Queen shouted at her son. "They will dispose of you the moment they have control of me."

"No, we won't," Jay said. "Asar is one of us now."

"You lie! He is my son! His allegiance is with me!"

She pointed at Rain and sent a spike of pain right through the center of her brain, making her scream and curl up into the fetal position as her shields crumbled to nothing. She wanted to die now, wanted to end the agony...

Telepathic shields surrounded her, protecting her fragile consciousness. Now she couldn't tell where she, Asar, and Jay ended or began...

"What is happening?" the Queen screeched. "This is not *possible!*"

The equivalent of a telepathic sonic boom went off in the chamber, sending Asar and Jay to the floor with her into blackness.

12

JAY WAS THE FIRST TO REGAIN CONSCIOUSNESS AND DISCOVERED he was in a stone-floored room with Rain and Asar that had no natural light or windows. There was no furniture either, so he assumed he was back in the palace dungeons. When the Queen had turned the full power of her wrath on Rain, both he and Asar had leapt in to save her at exactly the same moment, which had infuriated the Queen.

Which meant he had to act fast and get moving before the Queen left the province, leaving them to rot and taking her secrets with her. Jay staggered to his knees, still reeling from the force of the telepathic blow the Queen had dealt them. If they hadn't all reacted instinctively to shield each other—

"Jay?"

He looked down to see Rain opening her now-bloodshot eyes.

"Are you okay?" Jay asked. Asar muttered something foul and rolled away into the darkness to puke and curse. "I need to get out of here, and find the Queen."

Rain reached out and grabbed his ankle. "We all do, so slow

down a minute. Let's do what you originally suggested and work through this *together*."

Jay hesitated, all his thoughts on the Queen. He wasn't a natural team player. He wanted to protect Rain and Asar, not lead them into further danger. Rain dug her nails into his flesh, making him wince.

"Come on, Jay! We somehow survived by working together. We can do it again."

"I'm not sure how we managed to temporarily block her, but it almost killed us." Asar joined the conversation, his voice rough. "The Queen's power is endless and unfettered."

"But she's never encountered a human like Jay before, has she?" Rain pointed out, "Or..." She went still, her eyes widening. "Us. *All* of us together."

Jay frowned, trying to clear his lingering headache. "What do you mean?"

"Us as a bonded triad," Rain said. "I mean what we could *become*."

"You want to take time to have sex before we wander off to get the Queen?" Jay said incredulously.

"Think about it." Rain sat up. "She doesn't know I can bond. With the three of us and your A.I., we will become something she's never encountered before."

"I do not understand any of this." Asar was now frowning at Rain. "My mother said you were not pure Neveks."

"She lied, or else Jay brought something new to the equation and released that ability in me." Rain shrugged.

For the first time Asar smiled, his heart in his eyes. Jay thought he was remarkably calm for a man who was at odds with his mother for the first time in his life.

"I would willingly give my life to protect you *now*, but bonding with you?" He put his hand over his heart. "That would be a miracle."

"Be careful what you wish for," Jay muttered as he wiped the sweat from his brow. It was incredibly hot in the airless room, and he had no idea how long they'd been in there.

"LESS THAN ONE EARTH HOUR," his A.I. helpfully reminded him, and he winced at the noise level.

"It's an interesting idea, Rain, especially if Asar is willing to go along with it, but remember." Jay tried to regain control of the conversation. "We don't have two days to bond, and neither Asar or I can be staggering wrecks by the time you finish with us and we have to face the Queen."

Rain bit her lip. "What if we ask your A.I. for an optimum shortcut to achieve the result we require?"

"CALCULATING."

Jay heaved a resigned sigh, sat back on the floor, and took off his clothes.

Asar blinked at him. "What are you *doing*?"

"You might as well get naked," Jay said. "If Rain is going super feral, she'll rip off anything that gets in her way. I'd rather not hunt your mother down nude."

"I am still not sure what I am getting myself into." Asar held Jay's gaze. "But I must say this. I do not want you to kill my mother."

"I get that." Jay nodded. "I don't intend to kill her. I just need answers to some very important questions. Rain's the one who wants to murder the woman."

Asar swung around to Rain. "Will *you* promise not to kill her?"

"I promise that I'll only go for her if she threatens your life or Jay's." Rain glanced from him to Jay. "Will that satisfy you?"

"I suppose it will have to." Asar stretched out his massive frame. "I doubt there is an answer that will satisfy me, but I appreciate your restraint."

"CALCULATION COMPLETED," the A.I. interrupted them. "THIS SHOULD BE ENTERTAINING."

Jay blinked as his internal computer apparently developed a

sense of humor at the worse time imaginable. The A.I. sent the information to all three of them, and Jay nodded. "Okay, that's doable. Let's go for it."

"Wait." Rain touched his arm. "When we form this bond, there is no breaking it until we die. Are you both willing to agree to that?" She took a quick breath. "And Jay, when we *are* bonded, I expect you to share exactly why you came to Neveks."

Jay scanned the two bruised and battered faces in front of him, and made a decision that suddenly felt remarkably easy. "I'll do that now if you like."

"There's not enough time." Rain's smile was shaky, but definitely there. "Let's begin."

ASAR GLANCED NERVOUSLY from Rain to Jay as he stripped off his tunic. He could sense no one around their prison, which was directly beneath the royal apartments. He dared not attempt to discover where his mother was. Knowing her well, he suspected she wasn't done with them yet and was simply plotting to deceive them and leave, presumably with them all dead. If Jay hadn't thrown his psychic energy over them, Asar was fairly certain he and Rain would be dead now. The faint remnants of his trust for his mother had died while he still lived. She was unstable, she was dangerous, and he would not allow her to kill Rain or Jay.

"I WILL MONITOR THE EXTREMITIES AND ALERT YOU IF NECESSARY."

Asar jumped as the A.I. answered his unspoken worry about their security.

"*Thank you.*" Asar sent a tentative thought back.

"YOU ARE WELCOME."

Jay held up his wrist, the soft skin exposed, and slashed a line across his flesh, wincing at the slight sting. "Here, Rain, start with this. I know how blood turns you on."

Mystified, Asar watched as Rain pressed her mouth to the faint scar and slowly inhaled before rubbing her face against Jay's hand and wrist like a feral animal marking its territory.

Then she stepped away and paced the small space. Something about her movements sent shivers of anticipation laced with a healthy dose of fear straight to Asar's groin. He inhaled sharply as his skin heated and his cock kicked up…

Jay was also breathing heavily, his expression guarded like a man who knew what was coming but couldn't decide whether he loved it or loathed it. He touched the side of his scarred throat and swallowed hard, one hand cradling his rapidly expanding shaft.

"Brace yourself my friend," Jay murmured. "She'll probably go for you first. New blood and all that."

Asar reluctantly turned back to Rain, who was literally changing shape before his horrified eyes. He'd heard the stories of a female bonding, but he'd never anticipated this blood-curdling mix of fear and compulsion. She made a low, growling sound and turned fully toward him.

"Dear Gods…" Asar whispered as he stumbled back and hit the wall. The grotesque statues in the inner temple where only he was allowed as the son of the Queen suddenly made horrific sense. *"The goddess in the flesh."*

Rain no longer looked female; her skin was scaled armor and glowed red, and her eyes had blackened and changed shape. Fangs protruded from her elongated jaw, and her fingers were now claws. His cock throbbed hard as she approached like a predator, and he couldn't look away.

Her thoughts crashed into his mind, and for a moment he almost panicked. He floundered into the unknown, almost drowning in her demands until his body responded to her, lust betraying him, wanting her so badly that it hurt not to have her.

"Yeah, think of it like that," Jay muttered somewhere in his consciousness. *"The sacrifice is worth it."*

Rain snarled and leapt for Asar, her fangs snapping close to his face until they settled into his throat, holding him like the prey he was. Clawed fingers closed around his cock and then she was pressing down on him, her body taking him in. His mind dissolved into the chaos of fucking and a desire to give her everything she wanted even if he died from it.

He braced his feet on the floor, offering more, giving her his whole body to devour at her pleasure like a sacrifice laid open on the altar—blood, seed, and mind all hers, all—

He climaxed so fast it hurt, making him cry out as her fangs entered his neck to savor his blood. Even as he fought to gather the fragments of his mind, she moved off him and went for Jay, who groaned and toppled over as she brought him to the floor.

Asar could only watch as Rain rode Jay, her hips rising and falling, her claws raking his torso with each demanding thrust. Even as he struggled to breathe, Asar's cock strained with need —he wanted more, wanted *everything.*

"Come here."

It was impossible to resist Rain's commanding tone. He was already crawling toward her before she finished her demand. With one smooth motion she flipped onto her back bringing Jay over her, one clawed foot pliantly squarely in his ass spreading his cheeks.

"Fuck him."

Such was her power over Asar that he didn't think to disobey.

"It's okay. Do it raw." That was Jay's desperate voice. *"I'll worry about it if we survive."*

Asar slathered as much come and spit on himself as he could manage—which was a lot, seeing as his cock was dripping with need—and eased inside Jay's tight ass. The instant connection between the three of them almost made his head explode. He set his jaw, fighting the need to come.

He yelped as Rain's claws raked him from shoulder to ass like brands of fire marking him, making him smell his own blood.

"Come and keep fucking."

Just the sound of her command had him obeying her. Each jet of come was forced out of him. He kept moving his hips, and was instantly hard again. It was easier now. He fucked Jay with his mind in some deep pit of sexual hell and desire that made him want to scream with the extreme pleasure and pain of it. But he couldn't stop. He'd die giving her everything she demanded. He would kill anyone who tried to prise him out of Jay and Rain's arms.

WHILE HE WAS COMING for the third time, Rain threw Asar off Jay as if he weighed nothing. He rolled onto the stone floor gasping, one hand wrapped around his still jerking cock. In her mind, the A.I. ticked down the necessities of her conquest of both males, keeping her just this side of sanity and stopping her from giving in to the primitive desire to play with and fondle and drain her males for as many days as she could.

She pushed Jay off her, too, and breathed hard through her nose, her claws curling with the scent of her conquests. The smell of come, need, and blood owned her right now and bound the men to her. Both males were breathing hard, their gazes trained on her, half-fearful, half-lustful. She liked both of those things. She arched her back and considered what she wanted next.

"TIME IS COMPLETE. TRIAD FORMED."

She growled deep in her throat as the A.I. spoke in her head.

What did that puny set of *nothing* know? It was her right to take these men for as long as she wanted them.

"REMEMBER YOUR MISSION. STAY ON TASK."

Rain's gaze lingered on the spectacular beauty of the two men who were both watching her intently. They needed to give her more. She *demanded* more.

Reaching over she grabbed hold of Jay's cock.

"*Rain...you can drain us both later, but now we must stop the Queen.*" Jay groaned.

She snarled and nipped the crown of his cock, making him jerk like a puppet.

"*Rain...*"

Asar added his calm voice to Jay's, and she forced herself to focus, taking deep breaths until she could look at the men and see them not as her private meal, but as two warriors she needed to fight alongside her.

"Okay." She eased back on her heels and breathed deeply, using the focusing techniques her mother had taught her to contain the beast within again. She wiggled her jaw as it reset to normal and watched her claws retract.

"Are you good?" Jay crouched in front of her, a goblet of water in his outstretched hand.

She managed to nod and then speak. "Yes. Thank you." She could barely bring herself to look at Asar. He must think her a monster.

She drank the water, draining the cup as newfound telepathic paths forged their way through the meld of their three minds, expanding her consciousness and bringing a strength of purpose that was astounding.

So much *power*...

Even the A.I. was embedding itself in her mind. That tactical ability to calculate odds and probabilities might give them the edge they needed to capture the Queen.

She blinked as Asar fell to his knees and kissed her hand. "Goddess."

"Not quite." Rain tried to ease out of his grip, but he held on. She couldn't avoid looking at the red gash her fangs had made in his skin and inhale the smell of their joining. The calmness of his spirit rolled over her, their minds in perfect harmony just as she had once dreamed of.

He looked up at her, his heart in his eyes. "I am yours, Princess. Blood and soul."

She hated to spoil the moment but she had to ask…

"What about your mother?"

He sighed. "She…has been behaving strangely this last year. Even before you arrived, I was considering whether to seek help from the Senate as to her well-being."

"Hopefully, we can restrain her and find out what's going on." Rain patted his hand, and he finally released her. She really could do without too much touching right at this moment. She needed to channel her lust into aggression. "What's the plan, Jay?"

Her other male grimaced as he splashed water from the jug over his battered torso and pulled on his clothes. "I don't have one."

"What?" Rain gawped at him. "You *always* have a plan. You were the one who wanted to get out of here first!"

Jay looked quizzical. "You and Asar just fucked my brains out. Forgive me if I'm not quite on point just yet."

Rain rolled her eyes. "You enjoyed it. Now what have you got?"

"Take the Queen alive and keep her that way until I can get her to the Senate."

"Then perhaps Asar can distract her while you knock her out or something?" Rain suggested. "Or both of us can distract her. Where is she now?"

"INNER TEMPLE."

Rain stiffened. *"Near my mother?"*

"AFFIRMATIVE."

"Then I know the quickest way to get to her." Rain approached the door. "Can one of you open this?"

13

As they pounded along the corridors, Rain noticed—in a detached fashion—how much faster she could run without losing her breath. Had some of Jay's physical enhancements found their way across their shared bond? It sounded too fantastic to be real, but she didn't have time to analyze what was going on while her life and those of her two males hung in the balance.

"This way." Asar spoke in her head. *"There is a secret entrance to the inner chamber."*

She glanced over at his grim face as he opened a concealed door in the stone and indicated a set of spiral steps. What must he be feeling when they were after his mother?

"It is all right." Asar touched her shoulder as she went past him. *"She needs to be stopped. I just don't want her to be killed."*

She nodded and unsheathed the dagger she'd taken from one of the downed security guards they'd met on the way. *"Jay? How do you want to approach this?"*

"I will try and reason with her," Asar spoke across them both. *"Maybe I can persuade her that she needs help."*

"*You can certainly try,*" Jay answered him. "*But just be on the safe side. Rain and I will be closing in on her as well. You got that?*"

"*I understand.*" Asar stopped in front of another door and operated the mechanism. The back of a large hanging tapestry shifted slightly in the breeze as he opened the secret door.. "*She is close now.*"

Jay grabbed them both by the upper arm, his pale eyes glinting like metal. "*Now listen up. She probably knows we're here already. Asar goes first. He tries to talk her down. You and I take his flanks, Rain. If either of us sees an opportunity to* bring *her down, we go for it. Block her thoughts as best as you can. Use each other.*"

Asar and Rain nodded, and Jay let go of them.

Rain waited until Asar and Jay went through the doorway, and then followed along behind. They were in the heart of the temple now, the place where the Queen had banished Rain all those years ago. Nothing had changed except the agitated voice coming from the Queen's inner sanctum

"Find it! I know it was written somewhere!"

"If you would just allow me, my Queen." Rain stiffened as she heard her mother's quiet voice. "Here is the prophecy you seek."

Silence fell as the three of them advanced closer to the archway. The Queen spoke again, her voice a mixture of alarm and venom.

"This cannot be true! *Three shall join with four and control the universe.* They cannot mean my son and those two outsiders!"

"My daughter is Neveks born," Alaya said. "You deprived her of her birthright. Was it to avoid this very prophecy? I remember you changed toward us around that time. And recently you tried to kill me to draw Rain back to my side. Why?"

Rain took a hasty step forward, and was yanked back by Jay, his expression grim. "*No. Let it play out.*"

Rain gave him a death glare, but stayed put.

"Your daughter was not a fit mate for my son."

Alaya laughed. "Your son thinks otherwise."

"He is a fool led by his cock, like most men."

Asar straightened, his mouth tightening. Rain guessed his mother really wasn't helping him want to return to her side.

"If the gods wish our children to bond, then there is nothing you can do about it."

"I am the Queen Goddess on this planet!"

"You *serve* the gods," Alaya reminded the Queen.

"They serve *me*, and soon I will increase my power so that no one, *no one*, including the Senate and that ridiculous female at Quoxor can stand against me."

Asar stepped into the room. "And how exactly do you plan on doing that, Mother?"

The Queen didn't seem surprised by his presence or inclined to flee, so Rain followed Jay and took up a position on the right. Her mother was unharmed and looked well aware of the dangers she faced.

"The Oracle at Quoxor is weak, my son. She almost died in that last Etruscan raid. She should be replaced."

"By *you*?" Asar shook his head. "You really are delusional, Mother. The Quoxor Oracle is invincible."

The Queen drew herself up to her full height. Her skin was giving off red sparks like cinders, and her eyes glowed silver. Rain shivered and focused on her telepathic shields.

"You doubt me, my son? Has that female poisoned your mind against your own *mother*?"

"I was already doubting you." Asar hesitated. "Your recent behavior has been troubling. Disappearing at festival times when your people need your wisdom, silence about where you have been and whom you have been meeting. Every single security officer I sent with you has no memory of what happened while they were away, or is now dead. Why is that? What are you trying to hide?"

Jay stepped directly in front of the Queen. "I think I know."

"You are a machine inhabiting a human skin," the Queen jeered. "Why would *anyone* listen to you?"

"Because I have the authority of the Senate to investigate this matter to its fullest extent." Jay bowed. "I will take you into custody and deliver you to the Senate for questioning."

She raised her chin, her gaze radiating fury. "You cannot lay hands on me! I am a *Queen*."

"But I can." Asar said. "I am more than willing to find out what's going on, and, as your head of security, I officially defer to the Pavlovan Senate on this matter."

The Queen pivoted and grabbed hold of Rain's mother, a ceremonial dagger inches from her throat.

"Stay back!"

"Mother…" Asar stretched out his hand. "This is ridiculous. You are defiling the temple with your actions. Please reconsider. If you are innocent, then you will get your chance to plead your case."

"You *dare* to judge me?" The Queen's gaze fastened on the bloody wound on Asar's neck. "By the Goddess! You bonded with her, didn't you? You absolute *fool*!"

Without warning, a swathe of pain almost knocked Rain from her feet. She clutched at her head, thinking it might explode, and saw Asar writhing in agony on the ground. Everything in the room took to the air in a swirling dance of energy and rage with the Queen at the center.

"You *doubt* me, my son?" The Queen smiled. "I gave you life. I can take it away from you."

The pain and pressure increased, making it hard to breathe, let alone think. Rain crawled toward Asar, desperate to hold him in her arms and give him her strength. She managed to reach him and found Jay already kneeling on his other side, his jaw set in a rigid line of pain.

"We can't let her win," Rain screamed through the rising sound of the wind. "Hold on to me and Asar."

She had no idea why, but the instant they joined physically, the noise abated. Asar moaned and opened his eyes.

Rain looked over at the Queen, the quiet center of the shrieking winds and locked gazes. Fire burned low in Rain's gut as she smiled. "You can't kill him, you bitch. He belongs to me now."

"No." The Queen briefly closed her eyes. "*NO!*"

Rain leapt forward, shoving her mother sideways from the Queen. "This ends *now*."

The slash of the Queen's dagger caught her face, and blood momentarily blinded her. By the time she'd wiped it away, the Queen had vanished.

"Dammit!" Rain snarled.

"You okay?" Jay handed her some torn off fabric from her mother's silk tunic. "She went down the stairs. Are you coming?"

"Is my mother all right?" Rain asked. "I'm sorry, I should've gone for the Queen first."

"You did the right thing." Asar managed to pull himself up using the altar. His face was gray. "Go. I will take care of your mother. Take my strength. What is left of it."

"Come on, Rain." Jay pointed down a dark stairway. "She went that way."

As Rain followed him down the stairs, she pressed hard on the wadded up fabric to stop the flow of blood.

"I WILL TEND TO YOUR WOUND. PROCEED."

Jay's A.I. was definitely an improvement in her life. She tucked the rag in her belt, and made sure she still had her dagger. Not that it would do her much good in this particular battle. She and Jay would have to overpower the Queen and protect their minds at the same time.

"*Any idea where this tunnel might lead?*" Jay asked her.

Before Rain could form a reply, the A.I. answered. "IT CLEARS THE TEMPLE GROUNDS, AND COMES TO THE SURFACE BY THE PERIMETER WALL."

"An escape tunnel, then."

"AFFIRMATIVE."

"Then we'd better increase our pace and catch her before she disappears into the wilderness."

For a while they followed the steep passageway without speaking. Rain kept one hand grazing the wall to stop from falling on the uneven paving.

"PICKING UP ENEMY TRANSMISSION."

Even as he replied, Jay kept running. *"Details?"*

"FROM THE QUEEN TO A SHIP ORBITING OUR PLANET."

"Etruscan?"

"PROBABLE, BUT I CANNOT CONFIRM."

"Why aren't you surprised by that?" Rain poked Jay in the back. "What the *hell* is going on?"

"The Senate suspects the Queen has been colluding with the Etruscans to overthrow the Oracle, overrun the Senate, and take control of the planet."

"What?" Rain grabbed his arm and forced him to stop. *"That's* why you came to Neveks?"

"Yes."

"Then why didn't you tell me goddamn earlier?"

He raised an eyebrow. "Because you didn't have the necessary security clearance."

"Fuck that, Jay." Rain scowled at him. "You and I are going to have a long discussion about trust in relationships when we get back. You suck."

"I know." He kissed her bloodied nose. "Let's focus on making sure it doesn't happen, okay?"

She increased her pace to keep up with him.

"SUSPECT IS 50 METERS AHEAD MOVING SLOWLY.

STILL COMMUNICATING WITH ENEMY. I AM BLOCKING TRANSMISSION AS BEST AS I CAN. HAVE INFORMED HIGH COMMAND. SUGGEST DO NOT USE TELEPATHIC COMMUNICATION BETWEEN YOU TO AVOID DETECTION. ROUTE QUESTIONS THROUGH ME. THE QUEEN CANNOT DESTROY ME UNLESS SHE KILLS YOU BOTH FIRST."

"UNDERSTOOD." Jay spoke out loud. "Let's do this."

He didn't need to glance back at Rain to know she was still following him, and would obey his A.I.. She was a warrior, and an all-around badass whom he'd trust in any fight. She'd also taken his revelation about the Queen's behavior quite well, but he suspected she'd come back to it later. Asar's thoughts melded with Jay's, agreeing with his assessment, and then Asar went silent, too, providing his power to protect their triad, but keeping it quiet.

Suddenly, all the torches lining the walls went out, leaving them in a blackness you could taste. Behind him Rain gasped and almost crashed into him. Jay activated his night vision, checked with his A.I. that Rain now had it as well, and kept going. If the Queen's ride was delayed, and High Command was onto her, all they had to do was stall her until help arrived.

Coldness shuddered through him, and his steps slowed as images of his dying mother pleading with him flashed across his mind.

"He's a killer, he almost murdered his own mother. He'll kill again with no remorse, as he has no heart and soul. He's a deadly, unlovable machine."

Jay's chest tightened, and he fought for breath as the faces of all the soldiers he'd encountered in combat crowded in on him. Men he'd killed simply because he'd taken the devil's bargain and become a machine. His mother was right. He didn't deserve to live. He was a monster. He should turn his weapon on himself—

"Jay." Someone shook his arm. "Stop it."

He tried to speak, but disgust crowded his throat. He shook his head, wanting to puke.

"Jay, she's trying to get at you. This is what she does." He winced as Rain's fingers dug into his arm. "She's messing with your head. She's using your own memories and fears against you. Don't let her win. *Please*, Jay."

He dropped his face into the crook of Rain's shoulder and just breathed her in until he regained some semblance of self.

"I am proud to share my triad with you. Don't forget that."

"AS AM I, AND YOUR MALE, ASAR."

Jay managed a choking laugh at that helpful intervention. It seemed his A.I. was developing some independent thoughts within the triad structure as well.

"Okay. I'm good now." He took a deep, cleansing breath. "Did she get you, too?"

"She already worked her magic on me when I was eighteen, remember? I found myself on a bus out of Neveks with nowhere to go, wanting to kill myself." Rain pressed her hand to his heart. "We have to stop her. We have to go on."

"Okay." Jay took a moment to rebuild his shields. "Let's do this."

He could sense the Queen's power now, like a huge predator crouched at bay and cornered in the darkness.

Dangerous.

"ILLUMINATION."

Jay held up his hand and his palm lit up just enough to display the end of the passageway. The Queen was fumbling with the door, her attention half over her shoulder. His A.I. told him that she'd used up a lot of energy attempting to defeat their triad. If he could muster his power this might be his only chance to bring her down.

Before she could attack him again, Jay dropped his shoulder and sprinted so fast everything became a blur. He brought the Queen down to the ground, his hands around her waist, and kept her there.

Rain ran up, out of breath, and handed him the torn-up, bloodied rag she'd been using on her head wound. He winced at the sight, but he had no other means of securing the Queen Goddess's wrists.

"You will regret this."

The Queen's quiet words, dripping with menace, drilled into his head.

"I don't think so." Reluctant to engage her in his mind, Jay spoke out loud and busied himself making sure the knot was tight. "I'll leave it up to the Senate to decide your innocence or guilt."

"PAVLOVAN SHUTTLE SETTING DOWN JUST OUTSIDE THE WALLS. ETRUSCAN SHIP MOVING OUT OF PREVIOUS ORBIT. SHALL I REVEAL OUR LOCATION TO SENATOR ASH?"

"Go ahead." Jay looked up at Rain. "Get that door open, will you?"

"Yes, sir." She was limping quite badly now. Her hair was wild and her face stained with dried blood, but she still looked beautiful to him.

"What do you think will happen to the people of Neveks if you deprive them of their Queen Goddess?" the Queen asked.

Jay shrugged. "Not my problem. Presumably someone will take over. Someone your Gods approve of."

"I cannot be killed so easily, human. My life span is long and my vengeance eternal."

Jay glared at her. "You've already fucked up the lives of the two people I care about most in this world. What the hell else can you do?"

"I can curse them. I can make sure that your so-called Triad is a living hell."

"Yeah, right." Jay's enhanced hearing picked up the crackle of transmissions from the Pavlovan ship.

Rain came back toward him. "They are coming over the wall."

"Tell him." The Queen looked up at Rain.

"Tell him what?"

"That I can curse you for all eternity."

Rain went still. "Don't do that."

"As if you could stop me." The Queen raised her eyes to the ceiling and her voice rang out. "Hear me my Gods, close to the living heart of your sacred temple. Hear your Queen. Send curses down on this unnatural Triad. Make it barren and spill over into hatred and conflict. Make them wish for death. Make them kill each other."

"*No,*" Rain fell to her knees, her face white. "*Please.*"

A flutter of wings behind them in the passageway made Jay jump, and the Queen smile victoriously. "See? The sacred bird of truth comes to me to seal our bargain."

The small golden bird flew around in a circle three times, and then alighted on Rain's shoulder.

Jay looked at the Queen, whose mouth hung open in shock.

"Come to me, bird. *I* am the Goddess!"

"Seems like the bird has made its choice," Jay murmured. "Maybe your Gods have finally forsaken you for being a lying, treacherous bitch."

He looked up as a familiar figure came through the outside door.

"Sir." He stood and saluted Kaiden. He was frowning—it was his usual expression, so Jay wasn't too worried. "I have the Queen in custody."

"So I see. I have a security team outside to take her to Pavlovan City to await trial. They are programmed to resist telepathic coercion." Kaiden gave him a look. "I'll speak to you later."

"Yes, sir. Thank you, sir." Aware that he'd cocked up everything he possibly could during the mission, Jay couldn't say he was looking forward to the debriefing. But Kaiden would at least give him credit for capturing the Queen alive—or Jay hoped he would.

There were two other males behind Kaiden. They paused at the doorway to allow the security team to go past them and pick up the Queen. She was babbling quietly to herself, her face white with shock.

The blond-haired man inclined his head an inch as the Queen went past him, but his expression wasn't kind, and the Queen ignored him.

The dark-haired, uniformed man wasn't quite so polite. "Good riddance, eh, Ash? She damn near killed us both with her plots."

"There is a long way to go to establish exactly what transpired." The senator leaned on his cane, his exquisite face thoughtful. "The Queen is still innocent until proven guilty."

His companion snorted and muttered something under his breath.

Jay saluted Senator Ash and Esca, the commander of special security forces, who were part of the same Triad. "We have spoken evidence of collusion, sir. The Queen admitted she wanted to dispose of the Oracle at Quoxor and rule in her place with the help of the Etruscans."

"Thank you, Captain Roberts." Ash turned toward Rain. "Will you introduce me to your companion?"

"This is retired military specialist Rain Datta, sir. She saved my life."

Rain looked terrified facing the two most powerful males on the planet, but managed to nod.

"Thank you for everything you have done." Ash shook her hand. "Your country is very grateful."

"Asar, the Queen's son, helped, too." Rain found her voice. "The Queen almost killed him in revenge."

"Noted. We will treat him as a friend," Ash said, his pale eyes twinkling. "If you have retired from the military, I suspect you have found a new career right here."

"Doing what?" Rain asked dubiously.

"The sacred bird of truth only comes to those who will serve her well." Ash pointed at the bird still sitting on her shoulder. "You are of the Queen's bloodline and will make a fine and worthy successor with your two consorts."

Rain went pale and started to sway. Jay hastened to take her hand. "You don't have to think about all that right now," he told her hastily. "Think about how much you're going to enjoy telling me off for keeping secrets from you."

"That was my fault." The dark-haired man patted Rain's shoulder. "Jay was following orders. Only four of us knew what we suspected about the Queen. No one else did. We had to find a way to get into Neveks and you were are only chance. Your male risked everything to help his adopted planet, and we thank him for that."

"I understand, sir," Rain said. "Perhaps I'll take it into consideration when we discuss the matter more fully."

"Unfortunately, we have to get back to the city." Esca grinned. "Or I might enjoy hearing the mighty Jay being raked over the coals by his female. Thank you both again." He put his hand on Senator Ash's shoulder. "Hopefully now we can live without the fear of an Etruscan invasion and go home to *our* female and our new child."

"For a while." Ash sighed. "I suspect the Etruscans will never quite go away." His smile was sweet as he bowed to Rain and Jay. "Thank you again. We will require your testimony in the Senate at some point, but consider yourself on leave for a few weeks." He paused. "Although, I would appreciate it if you and your Triad would stay here and stabilize the Neveks population. They will have many questions about the actions of their Queen."

"Yes, sir." Jay saluted both men. "I think we can do that. Asar is well-loved here and will know exactly how to approach the matter."

Jay took Rain's hand as the two men left, deep in conversation.

"Are you okay?" Jay asked cautiously.

"Not really."

"Do you want to go and find Asar and your mother and see if they are all right?"

"Yes." She tried to smile. "I suppose I have to start somewhere."

He turned back the way they had come and retraced his steps along the steep passageway. Just before they entered the Queen's inner sanctum, Rain stopped walking and tugged urgently on Jays' hand.

"Do you think he meant it?" Rain said.

"About you being the Queen's heir?" Jay asked. "Yes."

She wrinkled her nose. "But how could that be possible?"

"Maybe you should ask your mother. She's the keeper of the temple secrets. It certainly explains why she was so keen on getting rid of you." Jay drew her into the room where Asar and Alaya stood together at the Queen's desk.

"Thank the Gods." Asar came toward them and drew them both into a huge, comforting embrace. "Is my mother…safe?"

"Yes," Rain reassured him.

"That she plotted with our enemies the Etruscans to take down the Oracle at Quoxor is beyond belief." Asar sighed. "I knew something was wrong, but how could I have missed all the signs?"

"Because it sounds way too preposterous," Rain said firmly. "I wouldn't have believed it even if Jay *had* told me earlier."

"Good to know," Jay murmured. "Another point in my favor before you rip me to shreds and eat me alive."

"Our line of the family is distantly related to the Queen's," Rain's mother spoke up. "I think that is one of the reasons why she sent you away. She hated competition. The other concerns the prophecy she was searching for."

"*Three shall join with four and control the universe.*" Asar repeated the words, his finger placed under the script on the page. "I don't quite understand what it means in relation to us though, do you?"

Alaya smiled. "You are the first known Triad to contain all the tribes, Pavlovan, Neveks, and Hakron. You also added a new element of human."

"AND MACHINE."

Alaya jumped. "Yes, that might be part of it as well. Your offspring will be...*exceptional.*"

Rain took her mother's hand. "But how can I rule here when the Queen is still living? I'm a *soldier.* I have no idea how to behave, or—"

"We will work these matters out, my love. Perhaps it is time for a new order, with power spread across your Triad rather than centered in one person?" Alaya patted her hand. "I will consult with the Gods and the priestesses. There is no need for you to do anything except stay here with me and your males until your path is made clear."

Jay smiled at both of the women. "Your mother is correct. Our first priority must be to reassure the Neveks people and prevent panic."

"Then I will go and speak to those in the temple immediately." Alaya bowed and left the room.

"I can help with calming the population." Asar marked the page in the book of prophecy and closed it.

Jay raised an eyebrow. "Buddy, you're going to lead, not help. I'll take on your job as securities officer, and Rain can liaise between the temple and the council to make sure we're all on the same page."

"I will start right now." Asar nodded. "There has already been some consternation about the walls of Neveks being breeched by the Pavlovan military."

"WAIT." Rain held out her hand. "Thank you, Asar."

"For what, Princess?"

She met his amber eyes. "I know this must be difficult for you, but I have to ask. Can you *really* imagine me in your mother's place?"

Asar took his time to reply, his considering gaze traveling from her head to her toes and back again.

"Yes."

"That's it?" Rain asked

He shrugged. "Even when you left Neveks, in my thoughts you have always been above me. Being your mate and consort is simply a dream come true for me."

Behind her Jay snorted, but Rain ignored him.

"Do you really mean that?"

His smile slipped. "Seeing as I allowed my own mother to be captured rather than allow her to hurt you, I hope my loyalty is never in doubt."

Rain reached up and wrapped her arms around him. For a long moment their minds locked until she understood him at his core. His sorrow and anguish over the betrayal of his mother would never quite go away. She could only hope he'd learn to live with the memories and move onward with her and Jay.

"Thank you, my mate," Rain whispered.

"You are welcome, my Princess."

He bent his head to kiss her. She forgot about the pain in her cheek and the exhaustion trembling through her limbs, and luxuriated in the true sense of homecoming only Asar could have given her.

Eventually he raised his head, his cheeks flushed and his eyes narrowed. "I should go and carry out my duties before I forget what they are. There is much to accomplish."

"Yes. Thank you." Rain watched him turn toward the door. *"But don't forget to come and join me and Jay in bed tonight."*

He stopped walking, and looked back at her over his shoulder.

"I assume that is meant to be an incentive?"

She smiled at him. *"I don't always morph. Sometimes I just like sex."*

"Truth," Jay chimed in to the conversation. *"Just come to bed with us. I suspect we'll all fall asleep in a nanosecond."*

Asar was still smiling as he closed the door behind him, leaving Rain alone with Jay.

He walked over to a couch at one end of the room. "If you're going to shout at me, I think I'd better sit down."

Rain frowned at him. "Are you injured?"

"No, just battered physically and mentally." He sighed. "It's been quite a day."

She took the seat opposite and took a moment to set her thoughts in order. It had indeed been a chaotic, terrifying day.

"Did you deliberately pick me up at the transit center?"

He sat back and regarded her. "Yes, but it went much further than that. The whole thing was orchestrated to get you to notice me and let me accompany you to Neveks."

"What do you mean, all of it?"

"The canceled bus, the accident taking out half the transit center—me 'saving you.'" He shrugged. "All that."

"You—"

"After I saved you, you were supposed to fall into my arms with gratitude, but you simply got up, dusted yourself off, and left." His smile was wry. "I had to chase around looking for you and catch up. I also wasn't supposed to want to fuck your brains out." He met her gaze. "That definitely wasn't part of the plan. After we checked in to the motel, I tried to get out of the mission, but Kaiden said there was no one else, and I had to make the best of it."

"So you just lied to me and kept going?"

He sighed. "I know it sounds bad, but I had this vitally important mission that I had to complete. Even though I was totally fucking things up I *had* to keep going. Only four people knew that there was someone leaking important Pavlovan secrets to the Etruscans. By a process of elimination, and the discreet dropping of a few false trails, the intelligence committee narrowed it down to someone in the senate or at one of the temples. No one wanted to believe it could be the Queen Goddess of Neveks, but eventually she became the prime suspect."

"I was attracted to you as well, so you can't take all the blame," Rain said. "And, as a member of the military, I understand the need to follow orders."

"But it still hurts that I didn't trust you." Jay interrupted her. "I can't fix that. All I can say is that it almost tore me apart. What you said…about me knowingly coming to mate with you." He shoved a hand through his hair and raised his gaze to hers. "I didn't know. I promise you. But I can't discount the fact that *someone* higher up might have known about the prophecy, or reckoned we were meant to be together. If I find out I was manipulated, there will be hell to pay and you will be the first to know."

"Thank you." Rain nodded.

"I can only promise you that going forward, I will never

knowingly keep you out of my head again," Jay concluded.

Rain sat up straight. "Like you could keep me out, anyway. I *own* you."

"Yeah, you do. Body and soul." He hesitated. "I'd given up on emotion. I thought I was too cold and lacking to ever merit anyone's love or attention. It's hard for me to trust anyone, but with you and Asar? I think I'm getting better at it."

"I'll keep you in line," Rain agreed.

"I goddamn hope so," Jay said so fervently that tears sprang into Rain's eyes. "I intend to behave myself from now on."

"You'd better, or else I'll eat you."

"There is that." He got off the couch and came to kneel at her feet. "I want you, Rain Datta. I…*need* you. Will you give me a chance?"

"If you'll give me one."

Rain took his hands in hers and noticed they were both trembling. All three of them needed each other. If she had her way, they would grow in confidence together until none of them would ever doubt they were loved and cherished for the rest of their lives.

"What can I do for you, Princess?" Jay asked, his pale blue eyes glittering.

"Support me through this…mess," Rain said in a rush. "I don't know if I want to be a queen, or whether I can rule over the Neveks people. It's all just ridiculous and scary at the moment."

"Asar and I will both be there for you." Jay paused. "You don't have to do anything you don't want to. Whatever you decide, or whatever the fates decide, you won't lose Asar or me. I can guarantee that. We love you. We are yours."

Rain cleared her throat hard as tears threatened. She was too tired to cry and had too much to do.

In one swift motion, Jay rose to his feet and picked her up in his arms.

"What are you *doing?*"

"Taking you to bed."

She punched his shoulder. "We don't have *time for* that right now."

Jay kicked open the door and marched down the hallway toward her bedroom. "Says the woman who insisted on having a bonding ceremony in the middle of a pursuit."

"That was necessary and probably saved our lives!" Rain protested as he dumped her unceremoniously on the bed and grinned down at her.

"Agreed, and we're not going to have sex. You're going to sleep, and I'm going to help Asar." He winked at her. "You'll need all your strength when we both come to you tonight."

Rain glared at him, and he held up his hands. "Just sleep, okay? We both know you're the boss in bed. Come and find us earlier if you want to help."

He went out again before Rain could argue with him more. She considered chasing him down, but her bed was so soft, and she was exhausted.

Tomorrow would be soon enough to work out what the hell she was meant to be doing for the rest of her life…

From being banished, to becoming a soldier, and now, possibly, a Queen Goddess.

Rain laughed out loud until she cried. How ridiculous was that?

But somehow along the way she had been blessed to find the two perfect males for her. She'd also discovered her powers. With a smile, Rain closed her eyes. For once in her life, she'd enjoy the quietness around her before her life changed again, possibly forever.

Except this time, she would be the one in control of her destiny, and she would no longer be alone.

The End

A NOTE TO READERS

Dear Readers,

There's nothing quite as entertaining in romancelandia as seeing a big strong Alpha Male brought to his knees. In this case, it's super-soldier and ice cold killer, Captain Jay Roberts, late of Planet Earth, and now on Pavlovan. He has no idea what he's dealing with when he tangles with Rain Datta who was banished from Neveks province on her 18th birthday and is now set to return and cause havoc. Rain has a mind of her own and a secret Jay will unlock that changes everything.

If you enjoyed this book, please consider leaving a review at your favorite retailer.

If you want to read more of my books, please check out my website and consider joining my newsletter for the fastest updates and early contests to win new books.

katepearce.com/newsletter

Thank you for reading!
Kate Pearce

Prologue

Somewhere in deep space
Earth year 2406
Hammersford Village, Planet Valhalla

"By Thor's bones, how old is she?"

King Marcus Blood Axe stared in disbelief at the girl the village elders of Hammersford ushered into his tent.

One of the men stepped forward. "She is of age, Sire. She is eighteen."

Marcus walked a slow circle around the woman. She wore nothing but a heavy gold chain around her neck. Her lips and nipples were rouged; black kohl edged her wide, scared eyes. He took her chin in his fingers and made her look at him.

"Do you want to have sex with me?"

She blinked and peered over Marcus' shoulder at the group of men behind him. "I wish to help my village, Sire. I wish to bring favor to our region by bearing your child." She sank to her knees and handed him an ancient gold goblet filled with thick crimson wine.

Marcus stared at her bowed head. Despite her beauty, his cock remained unimpressed. How was he supposed to bed her if he couldn't even get hard? He'd grown weary of this endless game. At first, he'd enjoyed being offered the most beautiful of his people's women but now, at thirty-five, he felt old, tired and jaded.

He turned and bowed to the anxious men behind him. He had no choice. Ritual demanded he play his part. The village was barely surviving on the edge of the Purple Desert. He had to give them hope. He drank deeply from the goblet of wine, wincing at the bitter aftertaste.

"I accept your gift and give you thanks for it. If this woman should bear my child, she and her village will be honored for all eternity."

The ritual words sounded hollow on his tongue as the men bowed their way out of his tent. He gestured reluctantly to the woman who knelt at his feet.

"Please, get up."

She stood, hands clasped together at her waist. Long brown hair curled to her hips and her head was adorned with a wreath of flowers. Marcus sat down and finished off the wine. He patted his knee. By Odin, he might as well get it over with. "Would you like to sit here?"

She nodded and came toward him, her breasts bounced as she walked. She balanced easily on his muscled thigh, one small, hot hand braced on his naked shoulder. He smoothed his hand down her back and she trembled like a frightened mare. Outside, the wind gathered speed, making the leather and silk hangings of the tent shudder and shake like a live animal.

"What is your name?"

"It is Lillian, Sire."

A beautiful name for a beautiful girl. Despite her age, he found it difficult to think of her as a woman. He understood why the village offered him their most prized possessions, their desire to enjoy the king's favor was reasonable. As rulers of the planet, his family held the ancient right to mate with any offered female and marry them if they proved fertile. Some of his ancestors had many wives. In more recent times, as fertile women proved elusive, they had difficulty in finding even one.

Lillian stared over his shoulder, her face a bland mask. He'd never really thought about how the women who were chosen to be bedded by the king felt about it. In his younger days he'd been too busy enjoying them to care.

Marcus licked his lips as his vision wavered. Lillian watched him through lowered eyelashes. A surge of heat settled in his belly and spread to his loins. Had the elders added an aphrodisiac to the cup? Did they believe the rumors that their king was impotent?

His cock hardened against her thigh. He barely resisted the impulse to rub himself against her. He slid his fingers into her hair.

"What was in the wine?"

"Only herbs to heighten your enjoyment, Sire, nothing more." He stared at her trembling mouth, wondered how his cock would feel as he thrust inside it. After a deep shuddering breath, which did nothing to calm the racing of his heart, he lifted her off his lap and set her away from him.

"Go, little one, I don't want to hurt you."

She fell to her knees and pressed her face to his thigh. "Please take me, I can't stand the shame if you leave me untouched. I'd rather face your anger if I fail to give you a child."

Marcus ripped open his loincloth and wrapped his fist around his cock. He squeezed hard, trying to restrain the raging desire to fuck her hard and fast. "What are you saying? Do you think I am a monster?"

"Everyone knows that you kill any woman who doesn't conceive your child." Lillian was crying so hard now that it was difficult for Marcus to make out her words. His gaze fell to her breasts which quivered with the force of her sobs. He sat back in his chair and pushed her away with his foot.

"I'm no monster. Leave me in peace." He desperately needed to attend to his cock before he came like an inexperienced boy.

Lillian got up and stood over him. Her tears had miraculously ceased. Her face was set. She placed her hands on the arms of his chair. The scent of her desperation and fear surrounded him.

"I'm not going anywhere."

Marcus' head fell back as she scrambled onto his lap, trapping him in the chair. She knelt over him and grabbed his cock. He could do nothing but groan as his body lost touch with reality and felt only the burning need to fornicate like a wild animal. He started to come as soon as she tried to lower herself down on him. His last thought as he lost consciousness was rage at being outwitted by a frightened woman and deep relief that he'd finally been allowed to spend his seed.

End of Sample

To continue reading, be sure to pick up Planet Mail at your favorite retailer.

ALSO BY KATE PEARCE

FOR A FULL LIST PLEASE GO TO KATEPEARCE.COM/BOOKS

The Diable Delamere Series

Historical Romance

Regency dukes, disinherited aristocrats and a plot to assassinate the Prince Regent create plenty of problems for all the heroes and heroines as they struggle to trust each other in an ever-changing game of love, deceit and treachery.

.

The Millcastle Series

Historical Romance

On the cusp of the industrial revolution in the northern town of Millcastle the old and the new clash both in matters of business and of the heart. Can love flourish among the rush to make a profit?

.

House of Pleasure / Simply Series

Historical Erotic Romance

Enter a Regency house of pleasure where nothing is forbidden and every sexual desire you have ever imagined can come true...

.

The Sinners Club

Historical Erotic Romance

When intrigue collides with heated passion behind the closed doors of the Sinners Club there is nowhere left to hide.

.

The Morgan Ranch Series

Contemporary Western Romance

A Northern Californian ranching family torn apart by tragedy reluctantly return home to discover not everything was as they thought it was, and that love, and forgiveness can sometimes go hand in hand.

.

The Millers of Morgan Valley Series

Contemporary Western Romance

When the mother you haven't seen for twenty years asks to visit your family ranch and set the record straight, how will her ex and six adult children react? The loves and sometimes messy lives of a ranching family.

.

The Turner Brothers

Contemporary Erotic Western Romance

Three half-brothers find their own uniquely passionate ways to find the loves of their lives and accept exactly who they are—no holds barred.

.

The Obsidian Series

Sci-Fi Romance

Join a renegade band of telepaths roaming the galaxy to protect and rescue their race from the evil empire intent on destroying them.

.

Planet Valhalla Series

Sci-Fi/Futuristic Erotic Romance

One human female crash lands on a planet full of men descended from the Vikings, one of whom is the King who claims her as his mate—what could possibly go wrong? A sexy romp through the stars with excessive sex, a touch of humor and some very satisfied women…

.

The Triad Series

Sci-Fi/Futuristic Erotic Romance

Welcome to an imaginary world where civilizations, clash against the new and unknown, where telepaths are revered and reviled, and where your destiny can be preordained by a living oracle. Add in a group of super-soldier telepaths rescued from Earth and forming sexual triads for life becomes even more complex and life changing.

.

The Tribute Series

Sci-Fi/Futuristic *Dark* Erotic Romance

To save their planet from extinction the government will demand everything from the condemned few—willingly or not.

"Fans of no-holds-barred erotic portrayals of non- and quasi-consensual encounters will devour this steamy triptych."

– Publishers Weekly

.

Soul Justice Series

Paranormal Romance

Come and join a San Francisco based secret government department who investigate the monsters under the bed while risking their psychic abilities and even their own lives.

.

Kurland St. Mary Mysteries

Historical Mystery

Writing as Catherine Lloyd

Join wounded cavalry hero Major Sir Robert Kurland and Lucy Harrington the rector's eldest daughter as they solve crimes in their quiet little village and gradually learn to appreciate each other.

ABOUT KATE PEARCE

New York Times and *USA Today* bestselling author Kate Pearce was born in England in the middle of a large family of girls and quickly found that her imagination was far more interesting than real life. After acquiring a degree in history and barely escaping from the British Civil Service alive, she moved to California and then to Hawaii with her kids and her husband and set about reinventing herself as a romance writer.

She is known for both her unconventional heroes and her joy at subverting romance clichés. In her spare time she self publishes science fiction erotic romance, historical romance, and whatever else she can imagine. You can find Kate at katepearce.com.

amazon.com/author/katepearce
goodreads.com/katepearce
bookbub.com/authors/kate-pearce
facebook.com/KatePearceAuthor
twitter.com/kate4queen

www.ingramcontent.com/pod-product-compliance
Lightning Source LLC
Chambersburg PA
CBHW030636190726

48286CB00008B/2538